Miasma

◆

Ω

Credits

Story: Guy Maybriar
Front & Back Cover Art: Mark Cooper
Interior Art: Ron Root (01-08)
Interior Art: Tatong Jurolan (09-10)
Interior Art: Shawn Langley (Elizabeth & Hanayo: Broken)
Interior Art: David Hernandez (L.P.T)
Cover Alteration: Guy Maybriar
Editor: Sarah

Contents

♦

Introduction

...Jesus Christ, I'm still alive. This is my third story, and still I am...alive. OK...let's go through some more events that occurred since 'Brother Roman', along with new revelations.

October 5th, 2019 is a night I have been thinking about for a long time. Very simple really: I almost cracked in two. Too much caffeine and guarana, cocktailed with sitting in one place for eight hours, caused some serious panicking inside my head. Never have I dug so deep into hidden memories, and rational thought left the building, bringing in waves of ideas that would only bring harm to myself. Thankfully, after chugging a gallon of cold water, the thoughts ceased.

Still, I wonder. Still, I wait. Why am I still here? The latest revelation that came across my desk was finding out from my mother that I was born as a mistake. She said it very bluntly with a chuckle (no eye contact) and proceeded about her current business. Later, I confronted her about it and she apologized, but in reality, I knew it all along. I did not mind the revelation; I just simply hated the approach. We have an extremely weird relationship; it is a combination of estranged and long-distance friends.

Speaking of friends, my best friend has gone silent. We have known each other since birth (30+ years), and I cannot get in touch with him. We haven't talked since December 2019, I fear I lost him forever.

I'm all alone now...something many people wanted for me: Ex-Stepfather, Ex-Lover, Ex...Ex...Ex...Ex...

I'm trying to keep it together still. I've descended into the music scene more now. From October 2019 to now (May 2020), I've listened to copious amounts of the following: Type-O Negative, Opeth, Porcupine Tree, Devin Townsend, Trivium, Deftones, Igorrr, & Ihsahn. As of late, I have dug more into synthwave/metal (Trevor Something, TimeCop1983,

LazerHawk, & Dance with the Dead), a multitude of post-rock (There's a Light, Aural Method, Distant Dream, The Last Sighs of the Wind, False Horizon, Cloudkicker, & Sonic Black Holes), Aran Tomoko, ambience (How to Disappear Completely), folk (The Pilgrim), and even discovered dungeon-synth!

One band, however, has marinated my greys that I can NEVER get enough of: Numenorean. Their album, 'Adore' did something unnatural to me when the track 'Horizon' came on. Their previous album, 'Home' did something similar to me when I heard the title track – don't get me started with Devour & Adore's title track.

See? I feel a little better now, I know I always write the same song & dance, but I'm still learning how to walk again, the crawling phase is going to take some time to get over.

Although, I feel I'm one of those few cats that has been handling this Covid-19 pandemic pretty great. I have witnessed some troubling events from people who state they're more "level-headed" than I. I mean, holy crap, I understand the situation, but some of these "normies" have drenched themselves in alcohol to the point where I saw one guy have his skin to the point of peeling! His exact words, "I could just bathe in this stuff!"

…I am prone to panic as well, but this is too much. I forgot my mask once and an old lady screamed at me for it. I placed it on later and proceeded to tell her that now all we have to worry about are fecal matter from the cesspool streets of New York (How could anyone love this state? I have hated it since birth; it's pure filth and the people are just as bad!), violence from every corner, police brutality, unemployment, drugs, hate, rape, corruption, every other disease that hasn't gone away, and of course suicide!

We live in a world of plenty, and still we behave like our ancestors; greedy disoriented meat factories.

I think what bothers me most is the fact that 'Deaths of Despair' are increasing, and "supposedly" we are all "#AloneTogether".

As an introvert I can tell you we are not in this together because those that preach the opposite have plenty of company to surround themselves with, and they are handling this as the end of times.

Meanwhile, people who are much more depressed than I are suffering continuously in silence; shrugged off and ignored! Maybe they would like to be invited to your party and mingle with others or go out for drinks after work instead of going straight home to an empty house where even the ghosts don't come to haunt.

If you are suffering alone, know that I am as well, just find your outlet and don't force yourself to do anything you don't want to do. Ease yourself to new experiences, people, hobbies, etc.

I'm rooting for you, don't let the silence of the early AM hours creep twisted thoughts into your head.

You.Have.Value
You.Have.Purpose
You.Are.Wonderful

Let's get this new fun started, I got the idea for this story back in 2014, started to write on 02/18/19, stopped briefly due to mental reasons, and finished on 05/01/20.

I did finish the first draft of my next story awhile back so October 2020 should run smoothly. The artist I'm currently working with has been nothing, but the best!

Stay well, behave yourself, hydrate, sleep properly, eat right, and try not to stress too much. I'm sending you a hug!

With all my love,
R.K. aka "Guy Mayriar"

Prologue

≈

The leached soil of iron was blessed with more natural minerals to add to its reddish hue. Through wild trees and sharp rocks, one by one they fell. A night like this echoed with their screams into the wild. The Guardian would not let them run with the item; it was his only purpose. What started with five whittled down to four.

They stumbled upon it unknowingly, but they would take it to sell in the Market. It would make them rich and bring them fame, and yet…none would make it to the base of the waterfall. The gushing water that fell down the cascade was christened with each member's blood. Where was the trail to help illuminate the way to home? Four had now become three.

On nights like this, the stars would provide little signals to enhance copulation between lovers in this climate. No need to keep your voice low….animals in heat can vocalize loudly through their mating rituals here. Too bad these specimens were prey for the blind Guardian. Three souls lost, and another to this predator.

One boy, one girl, and one savage to be each other's company this night. The Guardian was never alone; creatures of the land gave it aid. The young man lost his head to a companion of gargantuan pincers. Behold his Emperor, a sentinel with one eye and an erratic stinger. Little by little, muscle fibers were strewn apart. The venom had liquefied the rest for consumption. If only she had dropped the stolen item, but fear paralyzed the senses.

Alas, never has one witnessed this form of unnatural terror. She stood at the top of the waterfall; too slippery and hazardous to jump. What other choice did she have? The danger of hesitation got the better of her…the Guardian fell upon his last prey. She screamed, she kicked, and she even stabbed him with the knife on his person to escape his grasp.

A blue gas vented outward and her nostrils inhaled its pungent fumes. There were no more screams, no more kicks, and no more horror, just the moonlight shimmering across the Guardian's grotesque features. The skittering of the centipede across his face lifted off to reveal no eyes. It plunged deep to pull out a window to the soul, an offering for stealing his fetish. His Emperor returned to his back, all while placing the fetish back in its rightful owners' stitched hands – small, but growing from years of absorbing the nature of roots. For the next hour, a slow dissection of her body proceeded.

Now there were none left, but the soft sounds of branches and soothing waters. In his mind, he had succeeded in what the masters had once ordered of him: Keep the treasure of Kpalimé safe from all natives and foreigners.

Chapter 1: Malaise

≈

A member of the "Big Hill" watched the sunrise over Goodhart Hall like any other day. Bored with her mundane classes, she silently yearned for something new. Matcha tea could only take her so far through the teachings.

"They told me I could find you by the Hall, watching the birth of the sun with a forlorn look. I honestly thought they were kidding, but you really do look like you're waiting for a lost lover to return from the sea." An older man said to the young woman.

She was too zoned out to look behind her; she continued standing there stone-faced.

"Mrs. Burke?" he asked, standing beside her.
"…It's Ms. Burke now. Oh…Mr. Ferguson, been awhile since I've seen you," she replied looking at him.
"Please forgive me, I did not know. I've been travelling abroad, doing my usual routine, and brought you a gift." He handed her a small box.

With little enthusiasm, she unveiled the item, simply staring at it.

"It's a singing bowl I've had restored. We found it near the Himalayas where I was excavating."
"Thanks…I guess," she replied.
"…The Buddhists use them in a multitude of ways. I hear 'sound therapy' is pretty useful for improving health and function."
"I did say thanks, right?"

"Yes...yes you did. Well, I also wanted to let you know that my team and I received our approval for doing some light work over in West Africa, and we need an archaeologist. Your name came up when I was making my way back to the States."

"The Director wants me on temporary leave...or so I have heard. I don't think I would be much help."

"I see, well if you change your mind, I will be around the campgrounds most of the day meeting with some old colleagues from the field. You can find me at the Old Library later, where I'll be talking with another joining me; beautiful infrastructure," he said as he exited.

The woman whose name was Elizabeth Burke was a graduate of Bryn Mawr who studied how humans manipulate their material environment and the cultures of past societies for clues about their lives. This knowledge garnered a Bachelor of Arts degree in Archaeology, a field she has passion for. Her twenties were ending on a sour note...and not from becoming a new divorcee.

Her face showed no emotion when examining the bowl. However, intrigue took hold when she tried to figure out the composition. Was there mercury in this? Maybe there were small traces of gold perhaps? Does it become one with antimony? Now she knew she would need some privacy to see if this item could provide any sort of relief.

Classes would not start for a while, and always being prepared prior, gave her ample time to 'talk' with the new 'therapist'. Secluding herself in Dalton Hall, the young woman was having second thoughts about trying this type of meditation. Her eyes still looked tired even as the sun began to pierce the windows. The rays of light revealed an inscription inside.

"It's Devangari...I can't read this unless...great. That was his plan." she sighed to herself.

His name was Michael Ferguson, a Doctor of Philosophy from Columbia U. His main question in life was, 'What does it mean to be human?' Therefore, he listened to his muse and learned that social and hard sciences, with that of humanities, can all communicate together within the same disciplinary tradition. In plain words, anthropology would call on him...along with the horrific phenomena.

Her tea turned cold, as well as her demeanor. With an annoyed frustration furrowing her brow, she surrendered to the moment and decided to hear him out. Some on campus waved to her, but she did not acknowledge them. Now, with the sun over the Library, determination grew inside her. She hoped the new flame would compete against his silver persuasion. Arriving inside, she saw him alongside a few others, including the Director.

"Good morning Ms. Burke, I hear from Mr. Ferguson that you are still undecided about going with him and Mr. Dunham. Care to elaborate?" the Director asked.

Arthur Dunham was the third wheel for the meal. In regards to threes, his favorite words were semantics, syntax, and phonology. He, a Master of Linguistics, and a degree from M.I.T., usually volunteered his expertise in the study of nature and structure of language...only to neglect morphology when screaming takes hold...

"I am still debating. With exams coming up I feel I should properly prepare my students." Ms. Burke answered.
"Your curriculum has not changed much, and this shows a lack of interest on your part. In addition, I have members of the staff tell me about your recent standoffish behavior to both them and the students. Your personal problems are seeping into your working habits, and frankly, I am having a hard time believing you would be much aid to our fellow scholars present. Which would also mean somewhere down the line, I might have to sus..." the Director said before being interrupted.

"If I may, but I do believe Ms. Burke would be nothing but a great addition to the party, and above all, infinitely beneficial." Ferguson stated aloud.

"I agree, plus she also keeps me in check with my verbose behavior when I become overwhelmed from new projects. It is probably why my recent crew was quick to send me off once I finished with the Ayia Sotira excavation," Arthur said with a laugh trying to break the tension.

The Director and Elizabeth locked eyes with each other. Cool behaviors showed, but enflamed auras surrounded them.

"So, would you like to hear about this fun excursion?" Ferguson asked Elizabeth.

"Thrill me…" was the reply.

***

Fated lives for these few lied in a country whose anthem was, "Land of our ancestors": Togo. They would travel to the Capital, Lomé, and meet with some of the locals. From Lomé, it would be an hour and a half travel to Mount Agou, the tallest mountain in the country. Recent findings showed that a manmade cascade exploded from the mountain. With it emerged new ruins that remain untouched…but not abandoned.

"Sounds to me like every other archaeologist out there who has the time and funding would have stripped out the place. How long has this finding been circulating for, and why is this your concern?" she asked.

"For starters, it hasn't been announced globally yet, and because of that I was approached by Echigoya Industries to excavate it. Supplies and funds are more than secure; it is just a matter of putting my own team together who can get in and out before it reaches other peers' ears. They need my answer today, and it would be nice to study new findings in peace."

"Oh god, not her Michael…was she getting her fingernails dirty in the Himalayas or having others do it for her? Don't answer that, I already know the answer," Elizabeth said, rolling her eyes.

"...She had one of her collectors in the Akodessewa Market who heard about the discovery from the locals. She is very serious on this matter since she flew in to tell me in person. Police investigated the area, and can't explain the opening since there were no signs of tools used to reveal it."

"As interesting as this sounds, last I remember the country was still going through nearly daily protests. What makes you think our mission won't come to a full halt upon arrival? Moreover, isn't it possible that someone has already raided the ruins already?"

"Ms. Uesugi has procured a security detail at the site. In addition, she paid some in the Republic to give us a clear path around any potential threats. I think our bases are covered."

"Please don't say her name..."

"Ms. Burke, we need your professionalism for this. If that is too much to ask for we won't push this matter on you any longer. If you're onboard, however, all you need to do is sign the contracts."

Ms. Burke made no effort to reply.

"Come on Liz, fresh history to dig up. God knows what we'll find!" Arthur chimed in.

While they all waited for an answer, myriads of thoughts were churning through Ms. Burke's head.

Why did you take up this study of talent? Was it because you were different from the other girls growing up, and Mesa Verde National Park became your go-to for fun? Did you too want to find other coins of the past like Guy Mellgren discovered? Or...was it because your 'best friend' was going to relocate, and you couldn't handle the separation? Passion for you was work for him.

The knot is no longer tied; you are tired of tea, tired of the mundane, and especially tired of your passion now becoming work. Your hair has been down for too long, isn't it time you return to the dig? Do you really want to retire as some sort of curmudgeon? Then you yourself will become a relic of yesteryear. Except your ruin is the damp earth, and your public display is a tombstone: Here lies Elizabeth Burke: A good friend.

How boring...you would have wasted your entire life for nothing: wasted years, wasted dawns. Chance of a lifetime within your grasp, reach out and grab hold of it! Just like the bowl still in your hands.

She stopped thinking to ask a question – a decision made.

"Will you tell me what's inscribed on this piece, Michael?"

"Only if you're willing to join us," came the swift reply.

Elizabeth approached a table, her name laid out on both paper and an electronic device – the contracts. She signed them without a care for reading the contents of the thick pages and small font.

"That's why I'm asking," she replied with a grin.

"Haha, I wasn't being serious you know, but I'm glad you're joining us. Director, do you have anything to add?"

"...None, I will have the paperwork submitted. I hope this trip will do you some good Ms. Burke," the Director said before walking away.

It was first victory attained.

"Great stuff Liz! And just think we got the red carpet set up for us! Our own security, residence in the best hotel, enough funds to last us for years, and we get to be the first ones in God knows how long to venture into this unknown!" Arthur exclaimed.

She paid no mind to Arthur's words; getting away from it all seemed like the best course of action: tabula rasa.

Handing the bowl to Ferguson, she waited with bated breath. His fingers traced along the rim producing a faint sound. Putting one hand into his satchel, he pulled out a puja stick and struck the bowl to show the idiophones true potential.

"It states, 'As you put on fresh new clothes and take off those you've worn, you will replace your body with a fresh one, newly born'; Chapter 2 from the Bhagavad Gita."

"…What would you have done with that stick if I didn't come at all?" she asked.

"Well, I am quite fond of cooking so I could always use a backup for my molcajete." He jested.

Surprisingly, she laughed at the witty remark. He handed her the items and insisted she give it a go.

"Ready to uncover more from the unknown?" he asked.

"Lovecraft once said that the oldest and strongest emotion of civilization is fear, and the oldest and strongest kind of fear is fear of the unknown. However, I do not believe in chthonic monsters that skulk in the shadows. Fuck yeah I'm ready."

And with her reply, she gonged on the bowl.

Chapter 2: Anxiety

≈

The trio had set out to Lomé, Togo.

"Man I'll never get used to these long flights!" Arthur blurted out in the airport.

"Come now, ten hours is not all that bad Art. Enough time to catch up on sleep and research especially," Ferguson replied.

Elizabeth grabbed her belongings from the conveyor belt, when she suddenly noticed an Asian man in a suit standing very close to her side.

"Jesus Christ! Does personal space not mean anything to you creep?!"

"My apologies Ms. Burke, but considering the situation I need to gather everyone ASAP as per my orders." He stated with a slight bow.

"You're with E.I.T no doubt. Is…is 'She' here also?" she asked looking around the terminal.

"Not at the moment, Uesugi-san will be joining us in a week's time. My name is Hifumi and will be acting in her place until she arrives. Shall we go?" he said grabbing her luggage.

"Hey jackass I'm not weak to carry my own bags!"

"Conserve as much energy as possible for excavation, again as per orders," he replied as they exited, his back still against her.

They were already off to a bad start and in the heat no less. A small limo waited outside with Ferguson and Dunham already in it. Ferguson pulled out some notes to look over while Dunham stared outside like a dog off the collar. It did not take long before the trio got to the hotel, which was widely regarded as the jewel of Lomé. The fact they arrived late in the day helped magnify the high-rises regal presence emitting its neon blue colors.

With the trio settling into their temporary apartments, Hifumi advised them to meet him in one of the restaurants to discuss the details. Elizabeth sat on the edge of her bed and stared outside. Usually excitement roiled at this point when a new project comes into her hands. After all, not too many get this kind of first class opportunity, but her eyes drifted into space without so much as a care. The moon presented itself in a large boastful way; if there was a city blackout, it would illuminate everything with ease.

Now standing in front of the window, the natural satellite's presence had a small cloud blocking part of it, her trance was broken from the celestial body. She thought it best to go downstairs so as not to keep the others waiting. Grabbing a few of her belongings, she wanted another look at the moon as she might be too engulfed with work to pay attention to anything else. Confusion brewed now when she noticed that what she thought was a cloud appeared to be a large bird.

As she narrowed her eyes to try to see what kind, the animal then directed its flight towards the hotel. Her eyes opened normally to notice it change heights, with it leveling to her window. Her oculars grew wide when she saw it started to speed up as if possessed by a rocket. Fright took over her when its presence outshined the moon and a piercing screech emitted from the cursed creature. Taking no chances, she ran for the door, slamming it. Several guests stared at her, each with the same thoughts: What could be troubling the girl running down the halls in a panic?

"Hey Liz, over here!" Arthur yelled out in the restaurant.

"Art, we need to work on your inside voice lad," Michael said to him.

When she approached the table, everyone saw panic in her eyes, a sweat on her brow, and breathing bordering on hyperventilation. The two immediately asked what the matter was. Since she had been in such a lax mood over the past several months, the lost expression of other emotions flooded her and only a fumble of words came out. All she could mutter was, 'Large Bird.'

"This region has a considerable amount of large birds, from the African open bill to Rüppell's griffon vulture, the latter of which we are trying desperately to conserve." Hifumi continued, "It was probably out looking for food."

"At this hour, no…it knew what it was doing," she replied.

"Starve any animal long enough and it'll hunt for food at any time. Would you prefer I send one of my men to guard your door all night?"

"No…that won't be necessary."

"Sorry to disappoint you, but it was going to be done anyway in case of anyone trying to interfere or steal your future findings. Again…as per orders given to me."

"Goddammit Michael!" she said turning to him.

"Sorry Liz, I just found this out myself before you arrived," he replied.

"All-inclusive with a plethora of cons…" she muttered.

"Ms. Burke, can we get down to why you are here instead of seeing it as some sort of vacation? I think Mr. Dunham is the only one so far who sees the work as R&R…"

"Not yet…" she said, stopping a waiter.

She had no time for bonjours as she made her first demand known. He quickly gave the request to the bartender and in what seemed to be mere seconds returned with a glass of top shelf whiskey, neat. She downed half the glass into her empty stomach.

"Now you can start."

"…How uncouth." Hifumi muttered in Japanese.

He pulled out his laptop, some documents, and several findings to pass around the table for examination. Small contingents of soldiers from the government currently patrolled the lower areas of the mountain to prevent civilian interference. The station at the summit had evacuated, but the villagers refused to leave; neither money nor coercion could change their minds, so they will be ignored so long as they do not interfere.

At the entrance of the ruins were E.I.Ts own security personnel to safeguard any who might slip past the base. Reports of water coming from the new cascade detail it glows at certain times of the night, but it had stopped abruptly. E.I.Ts scientists are still showing inconclusive information on the cause. All they could trace was phosphate deposits intermingling with an unidentified compound. There was talk to get anomalistics involved.

E.I.T made the discovery of a ripped map found several feet inside the entrance and went through extensive scans to determine its origin. It was later discovered to be a "Pascaartes", or simply a Dutch sea chart. It was too illegible to read most of it besides the three letters in the top corner: GWC.

A final piece discovered was presented to the party. The trio had looked at it with great speculation. It was an engraved photo of a woman posing and behind the art was the signature of C. Collins alongside the year, 1754. E.I.T was positive this Collins had been part of the Dutch West India Company as one of its engravers during the final years of the slave trade. Other than that, the rest of what remained to be discovered was now in the care of the trio. Hifumi would give them some local laborers in need of quick cash and a few of E.I.Ts own selection of scientists and security…all done off the books.

"You realize how illegal this is, right? You've asked us to fly down here just to now tell us that not only have you greased the local agency's palms, but you've started excavating and taking the findings without submitting them to the government? God knows what else you aren't telling us," Elizabeth said to Hifumi.

"I have to agree with Ms. Burke, this is highly unorthodox. The punishments seem to outweigh the rewards." Michael chimed in.

"And you couldn't give us notification before allowing us to travel for those god forsaken hours?" Arthur continued, finally showing some backbone.

"The current situation here has put the superiors in quick demand for financial support, E.I.T was more than happy to oblige should they look away from our activities at the site." Hifumi responded back.

"...You're using the civil unrest as a cover up," Elizabeth said.

She pulled out her phone to try to grab the next plane home, but was unable to. The same happened for Ferguson and Dunham; the three were bewildered as to why there was no service inside a 5-star hotel.

"Hey what gives man, how come you're able to get an outside line?" Arthur asked Hifumi.

"E.I.Ts own network satellite, the government has shut down the country's internet in an attempt to quell the protests. If you all decide to stay I can give you three access...limited of course."

"That's literally keeping us hostage, and did you not forget we can just use the hotel's phones to cab back to the airport? Are you that stupid?" Elizabeth barked.

"Before you arrived, I asked Mr. Ferguson if you read the contract associated with this venture. He told me you signed both contracts, not bothering to read either of them – something about getting out of your current position as quickly as possible. You could go back home, but one part of the contract states if said party leaves prematurely before completion, they must pay back everything that E.I.T has picked up on their tab. What were you saying about being stupid?"

Elizabeth had no reply.

"Would you like me to return you home, expensively indebted to us, to an academia that will most likely suspend or terminate your services?"

"Please Hifumi that is enough! We're all colleagues here after all, there's no need for cut-throat behavior," Michael said.

"It's fine..." Elizabeth said.

"But!"

"E.I.T is a business, and we all agreed to use our expertise as a return of investment."

"I misjudged you Ms. Burke, very astute like kaichou."

"What's that?" she asked.

"Ms. Uesugi, the chairman and I am kachou, the section chief. Her father, Ueusugi-sama, is shachou, or as you may call it, the company president. Now that the pleasantries are over, I shall retire for the night. Enjoy your dinners, on the house of course."

Elizabeth, however, snatched the photo of the young woman from the table before Hifumi stored it away in its protective case. She would never kowtow unless it was in her favor.

"I'll need to thoroughly examine this... for research of course," she said staring at him.

"That is out of the question."

"Why? What would you need this for? It'll be returned of course."

"That's not the issue."

"So...what is the issue...kachou?"

His shoulders tensed up and an eye twitched slightly. She could hear his breathing with more mutterings in his native tongue. Arthur accidently broke the silence by coughing. Hifumi smoothed his hair back, realigning his tie, and it was then he pointed to a dark purple strip on the back of it.

"That is the issue. It is not part of the photo. When we sent this out for testing, the handler scratched a part of it off which emitted a tiny gas…he was catatonic for several hours before he came back, disturbed, I might add. Uesugi-sama forbids the handling of this unless in a contained environment. No exceptions…"

"Then I walk, and you'll just have to deal with my payments in pennies," she replied, taking another sip from the glass.

Their eyes played a game of chicken as to see who submits first. Hifumi sucked his teeth and gave in. He pulled out his phone and made the call in the corner of the restaurant. The conversation was short, and even though none understood a word from the distance, his glares over his shoulder told the story. Elizabeth grinned and knew she had won. The other two could not enjoy the outcome as she did. Hifumi returned to the table with a grin.

"You may have the photo and…'research' it to your heart's content."

"So why are you grinning?" Arthur asked.

"Am I? Ah, yes, Uesugi-san has just informed me she plans to arrive sooner than she thought. She is extremely ecstatic to meet with you Ms. Burke. Kaichou insists the old relic be your property now and to consider it a late wedding gift for which she was not invited to.

She hopes you are most pleased now."

The very thought of her previous lover with a 'best-kept secret with curves', brought tears to her eyes. She clenched the bottleneck and ran upstairs with it and the photo, her tail between her legs, leaving Arthur and Michael as they argued with Hifumi for the unnecessary remarks.

***

The night was young, but to her it was over. Rain was in the forecast, the heavy spirit having no effect on calming her down or even showering her with lethargy.

The materials of abundance in her room tried its best to slow down the anxiety. Each fiber filament of the wool carpet struggling to massage the thousands of nerves of the soles was a misstep. The misting of bergamot upon her soft pillows to boost one's mood felt like lead balloons. As for the pillow-top mattress, crisp linen sheets, and downed duvet, they were all a sinking ship. Nothing but the square amber bottle could soothe her internal uproar. Her body was against the headboard, knees to the chest, with the photo in hand. Where was her Collins to engrave an image of her, she thought to herself. By this time, rain had arrived with seemingly impeccable timing.

With total disregard for the ancient item, droplets met the dark purple strip. A fizzle started, from purple to blue, emitting a gas…into a nostril or two.

Noxious were the fumes, conjuring images of gloom. She stood up from the bed, to calm her nerves and fix her head. The bathroom called to her being while vibrations in the air were now fit to be seen. Wave upon wave made her soul feel closer to the grave. Were these the spirits from the bottle to make the body throttle? Here were some shaking knees, with balance no longer a breeze. A pair of clammy hands went against the frame, she had no one but herself to blame.

Lights refused to turn on; will the floor hear her muddled song? Another try at the switch; sent a short burst of illumination…to reveal a mutilated Burke in the tub. There was blackout again and she was now holding her temples, hoping her brain doesn't go mental. Legs now buckled as she moved by her knuckle. She whimpered pitifully as she crawled, cast down, and unable to bawl. Could this terror show come with another painful blow?

Electronics beeped across her way, with the laptop jingling a message clear as day. A video chat in queue from no other, but her ex-lover was in point of view. Still unable to walk, she must strive to the desk via a humiliating crawl. One arm reached outward, but the floor pulled her inward. Digital memories streamed across her face, but again the floor wants to show her another place. From fiber to quicksand, there was a new world at hand.

Welcome disillusioned nomad to the new road...

Kneeling now in a pool of blood, Elizabeth was now inside a barely lit cave, but she was not alone. Before her eyes were a small band of men in tribal garbs. Each wore various animal skins with some wearing skulls of the dead creatures. Moreover, in their center stood a man tied to a broken column...his sternum broken open by one of the tribesman. Irregular sounds of high frequencies screeched from his very being. They bounced off the stoned walls, causing the stalagmites to crack, and ready to fall with its harsh weight.

Mutilated bats lay at his feet with similar split cavities, and a rich assortment of vibrant flowers around each cadaver.

Elizabeth found her voice again, only to use it at this most terrible event unfolding before her. All heads turned to her with curious eyes. Seconds seemed like decades with each stare, frozen in a puddle of gore. Vines emerged from the pool to hold her arms down. The torturer creaked slowly towards the prey, only to stop midway. The now deceased man had more screams from his slumped body...but not of his own flesh.

A burst outward exposed the ribs in splintered directions and from the flesh was several tendrils wriggling out; animated intestines. Purging from the remains was a mist of blues, greens, and purples much like the flowers. However, there were figures emerging behind the gas...three to be exact. Each a different shape, each was spontaneous in movement, each a silhouette in the vibrant gas, and all crept towards Elizabeth.

Magnificent spawns of terror were coming into sight. The chattering march of uncountable limbs, the terrible shrill cries of a martyr, the guttural grunts hiding behind barbaric pincers –this was where irregular heartbeats compose with the ugly. Her breaths could be seen, and so could a few dozen vines descending from the ceiling. Each with their tips pointing at her; each with their ends opening up to unveil bulbous sick eyes to stare at her. The tendrils in the pool took action once again by submerging her, just like how the carpet did. The tribesman and three figures did not move…they just watched her drown in the pool with dread across her face.

Welcome enchanted pilgrim to the new long path…where no turns are accepted. Become driftwood basking in the rays of the warm sun. Float in the brilliant blue as you please. Aqua levitates you; now please sit still Ms. Burke. Allow the first guest of phenomena to learn to embrace your vision.

Unreal, she thought, *I am in the middle of the sea. No islands or palm trees, just me. I just went from a sacrificial den of unholy denizens to a sparkling world of stillness. Was any of this real?*
The liquor…it must be…I am probably lying on the carpet having myself a nightmare. This part is probably me becoming sober. I cannot feel the water, but my leg itches. The arousal of my nerves is a sure sign of waking up, albeit with a hangover.

Thanks to stimuli brought on by an altered carnivore, the advancing of legs skittered to its destination: the breasts of Elizabeth.

Skittering from the water, and through her pants, the nimble creature revealed its upper body from the opening of her shirt. The revealing of sclera matched the horrific reveal of an enlarged centipede hovering above her face. Each segment wriggled like stitched eels trying to escape. Elizabeth screamed and tried to get it off her – as its mandibles tried to gouge her eyes. Every time she slapped away the creature into the water, it returned to her, larger and faster.

It grew large enough to wrap around her legs and submerge her. Her panic intensified, but she managed to injure the beast with a strong punch to its side, freeing herself from its grip. The multi-legged horror drowned into the depths. She splashed relentlessly trying to find something to hold. Still she saw nothing for miles in the sparkling sea…except a whale of a shadow that formed below her.

She made a final gasp for air before the shadow pulled her down instantly. It released her from its hold, but she was too far down to swim upwards for air. Death by drowning became imminent. She tried to reach the top, however the giant shadow came before her. Death would not come from aqua filled lungs, but from a centipede of grandiose size opening its mouth to devour her – whales were dwarfed. The sheer strength of the vortex enveloped her into its body.

The next road begins for the second guest.

The archeologist now became the struggler with torch in hand. Was this the belly of the beast, a small cave of dew and mud? The anxiety could not keep up with the tensions building inside her psyche. Where did this torch come from? Why did it produce only a foot of light? What were those scrapping noises she was hearing? With nails to the jagged walls within proximity, a small figure appeared before her, clear as mud. A set of cracked wood claws reached out for her, accompanied by distorted wailing.

Run jilted lover, the torch is beginning to leave you as well. With every step you take, the tiny demon doubles its own speed.

Error produced: you looked behind you.

Her head cracked into a jutting rock, bringing her knees to the ground and making her eyes hazy. Reclaiming the torch, it shone a dead end before her. There was nowhere to run now, but at least she had someone, or something, holding onto her shoulders. Its head murmured unknown sounds into her ears, and a claw extinguished the light.

From opaque caves to heavenly skies, a New World resident welcomed her to its trembling mountain peak.

A gale of snow became her surroundings now and below her, a tower of ice. A constant shake vibrated through every cell trying to keep balance of the kingdom. The wide-eyed struggler was doing well and her reward was a large turkey vulture to greet her. Having control of the thermals helped it encircle her with great speed. Her eyes tried to keep up with its presence until she realized the shaking became more pronounced. Chunks of the peak broke off leaving her less area to stand on. Thick clouds below her only signaled lies; *trust us to catch you.* 'Full speed ahead,' said the aerial ram, and now the thin cold air accompanied heartfelt screams.

Transformation plus disfiguration equated to the final guests for observation.

Her body smashed flat onto soft earth; what seemed like a drop from orbit turned to a fall of two feet.

Why do you turn on your side, crying in despair?
This is a part of your daily sanctuary: a nature trail engulfed by berry thickets, leaves, and bark of homeland Pennsylvania.
A cornucopia of dead leaves blanketed the trail and there was a sudden shuffle under them. Sights turned behind her to see the noise. From bursting mud, an enormous tail with an eye attached at the end grew out of the foliage. The vision found the struggler alongside the countless of branches leering at her with eyes protruding through each twisted stem.

This is your last chance at flight before you are doomed to losing the fight.
Can your feet keep up with your mind? Don't trip like some trashy horror movie character, this is no time to be stupid. Impending doom trails behind you. The rays of the sun are lost to the thick of the forest; the trail is losing distance to nothingness. You hear the sounds of heavy armor chasing after you, for the tail has emerged from mud to give birth to the black Emperor.

Turn your head and you lose speed and join those of the dead. But, is forward march the right way as well? Now the shuffling of limbs comes before you.

A full stop in tracks and the Emperor's noises disappeared for its leader gave rise from the darkness. Crooked limbs, tattered pants, sutured organs, hollowed eyes; for this was the captured man tortured and revised. Does one become ensnared by the zombie, torn bit-by-bit by the Emperor, or…run a new path to the side? Her feet reacting on their own, no stopping now, there were no other options.

The figure still standing in place watched her run into the distance, where does this lead? Her breath was almost out, but fortunately, the dead man remained. Fortune smiled but only briefly. A wooden child shrunk down, attaching to his waist. The slithering of a centipede embraced his crown to become personal eyes. Meanwhile the pincers of the emperor hugged his sides, shield and weapon to his back. Blasting over the trees to retrieve the unholy party, the vulture had grown twenty times its size. From New World to Old World, its transformation revealed a bearded one.

The bird of prey's wings trampled over trees – unyielding. The distance between Burke and her pursuers grew closer now. The undead man looked over his carrier to watch her run in vain, was it all a game? From her level to the sky, the vulture raced ahead of her. She noticed it was alone now…oh no, she thought. Her one-eighty degree showed the horrors soaring through the air towards her; knife in hand.

No time to breathe, no time to react with speed, only time to watch the demon's blade crush into your chest. Inches from your face, clenching his teeth, and exhaling a colorful mist into your lungs…you see the calling of fate.

Wakeup struggler from your nightmares and despairs, maybe this is all a warning to run away from sleeping bears.

Chapter 3: Revelation

≈

Hotel management did an over-ride on Elizabeth's access card panel only to see her lying across the floor. Michael and Arthur accompanied them. The residence was in perfect condition minus the large spill of whiskey on the sheets. Placing his hand on her neck, a strong pulse showed she had not submitted to alcohol poisoning much to Michael's relief. The hotel insisted she be taken into medical care as a precaution with the duo agreeing to this.

"No need…" she said, eyes still closed.
"Jesus, Liz are you ok? Most of the people on your floor heard you screaming for dear life not too long ago!" Arthur asked.
"Couldn't be…I'm too exhausted to move now let alone scream. I just had too much to drink from our dinner, now…go back to sleep."
"Liz, what time do you think it is?" Michael asked.

He helped her up onto a chair. A hotel worker brought her water, medicine, and a cool rag to ease her hangover. Arthur drew the curtains to expose daylight; no more drinking until this damned excavation was done.

"I swear I had just seen all of you not too long ago. No more drinks for a while, I'll just stick to my tea," she replied, popping the pill, "And screaming? I've been drunk before, but it never included loud behavior…well just once."

They tried to explain she let out screams of despair for the past ten minutes. Ten minutes of screaming and now from night to light in a matter of moments…too inconceivable, she thought. Looking at all parts of the room, she wondered where the old photo was displaced. Arthur pointed to the laptop; its monitor still up and the photo placed on it.

The colorful strip was still intact with just a small circle erasing a part, there were no more tears also. The duo thought she might need a day to rest while they went up ahead. She denounced the thought and after the nightmares she had, she became more eager to start this unorthodox project.

Everyone left the room for her to get herself in order. From shower to fresh clothes, she grabbed all the necessities to place in her backpack – slapping her cheeks to regain focus, it was time to go. With her hand hovering over the doorknob, her sights turned back to her laptop. She clicked a few keys to look at her video call history; it had been weeks since she had last received one. Telling herself that 'whatever happens, happens', she left to meet the team.

***

An enormous RV was their means of transportation to and from the dig site. Several bodyguards were inside with Hifumi leading the way. The trio became a bit unnerved when they started to realize that the dig site was becoming more and more suspicious. A small television showed where the protestors were concentrated. With only two routes to the mountain, the most violent group blocked the shortest. Eyadema Tsevie would be the only way.

The trio began to discuss the details with preparations and examining recent photos. The images that Elizabeth had witnessed showed numerous signs of tense body language; dissected animals, undocumented tribal practices, living homunculi…an unbalanced mind asking help from a higher power. She wanted to believe it was a dream from strong spirits and bad memories, just a synchronization of nightmare fuel.

That man though, who was he, better yet, what was he…?

"Did you have trouble sleeping, Ms. Burke?" Hifumi asked in his usual flat tone.

"Why ask if you already know the answer? It's too early for you."

"Very well, but I hope you have this much energy for the coming week."

"Surprised you didn't pop your head in the room, Mr. Update."

"No need besides having Ms. Uesugi notified about it. She'll arrive sooner now."

He could hear her groans from the front. Arthur tried to distract her with photos from his recent projects, each showing ridiculous facial expressions. Poker face would lose to laughing. Michael on the other hand was quiet. He simply wrote down notes in his travel journal, occasionally looking up to observe Hifumi, the security detail, and Elizabeth. He had a gut feeling too strong to ignore to which he wondered what the outcome would be. His biggest concern was Elizabeth and the strange behavior exhibited earlier.

The days were long, but the decades were short. This sunbathed land was withholding terrible secrets from the past...some of which were never buried.

Everyone had finally arrived at the base of the mountain in wait, staring out the window to observe their surroundings.

"Not as big as I imagined, the trail is only three miles to the summit," Arthur said.

"Where are the park officials?" Michael asked.

"Paid leave until we're done here, E.I.T has secured the entire mountain for ourselves – only a small amount of the government's own are allowed, and only at the base. Ms. Uesugi wanted little to no interference with the populace. Only a local supervisor is allowed with the others to show we would not be damaging the mountain; politics of course," Hifumi replied.

"Dirty money more like it," Elizabeth said under her breath.

Someone began knocking on the side of the door, an exterior camera showing it to be a large bald male in business attire. Hifumi nodded to one of the guards to open the door and in walked a man of goliath proportions. He stood over the trio, gazing at them with pitch-black glasses and an aura of peerless might. A hand that rivaled a bear's stood out to shake Michael's hand first. With a steel wire grip, the press commenced.

"My, you have quite the grip, don't you mister…?"

"Apologies, Carl Hughes. I am in charge of the security detachment. My men have been very anxious for all of you."

"And why is that, fans of anthropology?" Arthur asked.

"Far from it, they're damned near tired basking in this god forsaken weather and want to leave this hellhole. I myself included."

"Mr. Hughes has done quite well for us in the past, what with his previous military experience in the marines. You won't find a better man to make sure you three do your jobs uninterrupted," Hifumi said. "Now, make your way to the top with the jeep provided."

"Aren't you coming?" Arthur asked.

"…No, I have other business to attend to."

Michael made a mental note on his hesitation. The trio traveled to the top, anxious to see what had been uncovered.

＊＊

Meanwhile Hifumi spoke in private with Hughes still at the base.

"Your message said it was urgent, something you rarely throw around," Hifumi said to him.

"Right sir…and we have it quarantined," he replied leading the way.

A tent portraying a medical sign had several scientists waiting outside. There were explicit instructions given to enter with hazmat suits only. With their new outfits, the two entered the small space, greeted by one scientist and a recent finding.

"One of my patrols found it near the cascade, not too far from the sites entrance."

"…Are the villagers aware?" Hifumi asked.

"No, but if they knew we had this they would have us crucified and it'd put the company out of business; all of us jailed too if we're lucky."

"Yes, a scandal of this magnitude would definitely bring great shame to the family. If we are lucky, those three will not find any more of these. The woman especially would be the first to blow the whistle on us. Although…accidents can happen in archaic foundations, right Mr. Hughes?" Hifumi said, looking at Hughes.

"I'm already bought, why would I care?"

"Good, now…you, tell me why the need for the extra protection." He asked the scientist.

***

Familiar secrets were shared and even more questions asked. The hole to these findings kept growing deeper and deeper. Unknown myths clawed towards the sun, ready to eclipse the world, embarking to envelope everything with black fire. The masters watched everything from afar, everything going according to causality.

From the fire, he will uproot from the captivity of the land. The gaseous plague bearer awaiting new orders to plant new seeds for the forest must return…one body at a time…

***

The company of three reached the top to be greeted by other members from E.I.T. Michael talked with them to assess the situation, with Arthur taking pictures for the sake of memories, and Elizabeth observing the small entrance to the ruins. It was hard to believe there could even be ruins on this small mountain.

Those feint familiar mental whispers started their talks again. Unappealing visions giving rise to another tension-type headache (TTH). She hoped another pill would soothe the great throbbing thinker inside the cage, hoping to burst to freedom through the parietal, what a sight that would be for the grindhouse cinema. A swig from her canteen and a pinch on the bridge seemed best to control the moment. The strong heat intensified each beat of the drum; thank god, it was not the usual time of the month.

Looking back into the darkness proved that it too was looking back at her. Glowing prismatic eyes stared blankly at her. Flashbacks of the nightmares returning in nonlinear stages, preparing a great scream of anguish.

"Smile!" Arthur said to her, taking her picture.

The camera's flash broke her terrified trance.

"Liz, you alright?" he asked.

Her gaze went to him, and returned to the entrance…nothing there now. Still afraid to tell anyone about the hellish episode from the previous night, she tried to remain calm. They would call it complications of post-infidelity stress disorder (PISD), quickly dismissing it and reporting she had lost her knack for analyzing material culture.

A nod with a dose of another pill for the headache was her answer. Michael came over and placed his hand on her shoulder. She said she was all right, but he thought she was taking too many pills. He advised her to use the med-tent before venturing inside, and held out his hand. Reluctantly, she gave him the bottle of pills and proceeded with a physical. Hughes had now come to the top to meet them.

Inside the tent, E.I.T started a routine checkup, an elderly woman, who was the head doctor, checked out almost every part of Elizabeth's body. She was mortified by the situation considering her own healthcare practitioner never got this physical with her. The inspection of the abdomen area showed all organs were healthy, the stethoscope heard no abnormal sounds, and even the percussion test showed zero areas of unwanted fluid.

The doctor held up her small flashlight to inspect the eyes. Both reacted and constricted to the light equally, but she noticed one pupil was different in size. Taking a closer look, she briefly saw a thin wriggle inside. Trauma was ruled out and she believed Elizabeth had been infected with loiasis, but it seemed impossible. More diagnostics took place including a specialized blood test. Hughes entered the tent to ask why it was taking longer than usual.

Elizabeth shrieked at the sudden interruption of the large man considering she was half-naked. Michael and Arthur berated him, but they too were part of the interruption and included in the ejection. The doctor explained the situation to the three, outside. Michael and Arthur immediately wanted her to go to the hospital, but Hughes was quiet.

The doctor knew from his stone face that their employer was on the way and she would want results before arriving.

The doctor and Hughes talked in private, and Elizabeth came out to see the commotion. Michael informed her she might have contracted the disease possibly from one of the native flies. The doctor came over to state it was impossible given there were no visible signs of being bitten on her body, but that further study was needed.

Hughes at this time instructed that the three should start their work immediately despite hearing the alarming news. Arthur's carefree demeanor turned to barking guard at Hughes regardless if he overshadowed him. He instructed them that extensive medical treatment would be waiting for her upon their return to the city. E.I.T would ensure nothing would happen to any of them as per instructions from Ms. Uesugi. Antibiotics were given to the three, and now they would venture finally into the unknown.

Are you certain you do not believe in ancient beings stalking you in the blackness of perilous landscapes? What is evil after all? Maybe there is no such thing as morality; a construct for those that believe there is only one right way of thinking. Are monsters truly pernicious by nature, or do they just act according to instinct like starved animals? Is it possible they are warnings to prevent calamitous events?
Why are you thinking this way Elizabeth Burke?

***

"My God!" Michael exclaimed, the three unable to fathom the surrounding environment.

The trio were taken aback as it was impossible to understand. The reality of the situation could not be explained properly. A forest within a small mountain, even the cavernous ceilings appeared to resemble the night sky. A dilapidated temple towering above them and three archways, constructed into the earth, would lead towards the epicenter of it. Some of E.I.Ts engineers informed them that they had already searched the top to find nothing and they still were unsure the direct source of the explosive reveal to the entrance.

Elizabeth and the engineers all agreed that the local's ancestors did not do the construction of these ruins. Whoever constructed these stone formations had some sort of knowledge of Baroque architecture, as simple as it appeared. Too many questions, not enough answers; sparks of the nightmare shocked Elizabeth, these ruins greatly resembled the sacrificial chamber, but something was amiss. Even though E.I.T had taken the initiative on the project, everyone was still in the dark. There were no signs of the flowers she saw, and what's more, where was the water coming from and why did it stop now?

The trio worked alongside E.I.T for hours digging, sifting, measuring, and analyzing. Many trowels scraped away at thin layers of soil, hoping to find as much evidence of past human activity from the calcareous sediment. The vegetation contained abnormal amounts of sphagnum; what caused all of this peat moss? Arthur took copious amounts of pictures to study with the team hoping to locate something they might have overlooked.

The three archways all led to one large open area of stone and wall. Careful scans of the construction showed nothing behind each part. The open area was directly below the crumbling foundation. It was believed that maybe the locals had pilfered the ruins before E.I.T arrived. They had six more days before they were to pack up and leave. Everyone left after an exhausting day compiling and labeling everything examined. Only the security team would stay overnight.

The trio returned to the hotel, greeted by a specialist to accompany them and the head doctor to the hospital to evaluate everyone's health on the matter. E.I.T took a special interest in them, prioritizing their health above all else.

***

Blind eyes and foreign spies keeping watch from across the seas and nearby trees. Two generals at play, ready to cause a great skirmish of disarray. One eyes the prize, the other waits in disguise, sheep on the board and all in discord. Inanimate organism waiting to rend, and day one meets its end.

Chapter 4: Chimerical

≈

The trio returned the next day; all received a clean bill of health. Elizabeth underwent extensive diagnostics. Nothing was found from the ordinary, which greatly bewildered the head doctor. To be human is to err, she supposed.

They arrived to meet Hughes yelling orders to his men. From what they overheard, several men from the overnight security team had gone missing, and he suspected foul play despite no evidence found. The drive took longer to get to the site with the protestors growing larger now. They did not show any interest in their arrival, but nothing was ruled out yet. People going missing caused great concern considering they showed no signs of committing to desertion.

Still, there was the fulfillment of work and only so much time to do it. Hifumi kept tabs through Hughes, but considering the current climate he talked on the phone with Michael. A great exchange of bland dialogue between the two went on for some time. Michael, although quite the teacher, could tell he was starting to bore his receiver when going into the details of holism, cultural relativism, and emic and etic.

Unbeknownst to him, Hifumi showed no interest in this field whatsoever, even though he was part of these ordeals consistently. He only wanted results to please the voracious hunger of his materialistic employer.

Elizabeth scolded Michael for being too loud, telling him to take the conversation elsewhere in the large ruin. Isolating himself from the group, he continued his mundane talks with great passion.

His hands touched the hanging bits of moss from the stonework. He was too fascinated and still perplexed with this architecture buried in this mountain; did distant settlers make this a base at one point? He felt a jagged formation underneath one area and removed the blocking greenery. There he made his first discovery, a string of words he could not understand. Hifumi would translate for him.

"Sterker door strijd? Am I pronouncing that correctly?" he asked.

Hifumi asked for the spelling and left Michael waiting on the line to research this new discovery.
"It is Dutch; Rotterdam's motto: Stronger by struggle."

Small cloudy drippings from above landed on Michael's extended hand.

"What in the name of...?"

His head turned to the ceiling, but without a proper setup of lights, all he could see was pitch black. He heard something above him skittering about; his heart began its sprint.

"Did you discover something else?" Hifumi asked, hearing a change of breathing from the other end.
"Uh, no I just thought I heard some...agh!" he replied before gripping his hand in pain.

The phone dropped and Hifumi tried to get a hold of him from a distance. All the muscles in Michael's hand flexed with an extreme amount of pressure. The skittering noises heard from above grew louder now. Panic started to set in, was something stalking him from the darkness above?
Arthur heard his cries of pain and rushed over with great haste. He saw Michael on his knees, hunched over and holding his wrist. He saw the liquid and dumped his entire canteen of water to wash it off. He grabbed hold of him to bring him outside to the med tent. Michael insisted on using his camera's flash to illuminate above them.
The flash went off like a solar flare and he even held his own flashlight to search the stone ceiling, nothing of importance was seen. The pair informed Elizabeth of what had happened and the three made their exit.

***

Arthur, who was trying to delete the unimportant photos, noticed tracking on the stone surface. He sent them to Hifumi for his team to look over, but they too were confused. It was not because they did not know what it was, but because of the sheer size of each mark. Their suspicions were further confirmed when Michael was examined and they found a large amount of neurotoxins that could have caused necrosis in the muscles had Arthur not intervened sooner. His heart, however, beating irregularly and fast showed that the venom tried its best to cause a fatality. E.I.T was more than prepared for events such as these and considering their hunch of the species involved, the injected antivenin stopped Michael's brief, yet harsh, suffering.

Elizabeth and Arthur stayed by Michael's side in the tent. Meanwhile the head doctor, her assistants, and some of the scientists talked to Hughes regarding the situation, far from the trio. He did not like what he heard; they all considered this too dangerous and wanted an immediate evacuation. Just like the trio, they had contracts, but theirs were far more severe since they worked directly with the Company…too many secrets might go "missing" in these ruins from a collapsed wall…

Hughes himself thought the risks outweighed the rewards; he still could not locate some of his best that stayed for the overnight shift. Did they become like what they quarantined?

"We're getting him the hell out of here!" Elizabeth shouted, coming outside to disrupt the private conversation, "And there's no fucking way you're going to deny it! Or so help me!"

Hughes did not react – he stayed composed. He told the doctor her place was now at Michael's side for now, back at the hotel. More doctors and security were en route to the country anyway, this time he was sure things would go well since Hifumi promptly executed his request for more, especially after he witnessed Hughes' finding.

The trio left the site with the doctor and asked her what could have possibly bitten Michael. Hesitant, all she could say were the words 'telson' and 'Chelicerata'. Arthur knew the latter as "claw" and "horn", but not the former. Telson was the posterior-most division of the body found amongst certain insects, crustaceans, and the like that usually held toxins. He concluded from the venom and the pictures that it was a scorpion of unknown origin.

Images of the one-eyed extremity and hulking armor jolted through Elizabeth's mind, causing her to pop another pill. The doctor examined her eyes as a precaution, and discovered no anomalies.

None knew yet that this Pandinus once intermingled with Leiurus; a twisted means of justice via synthesis. Maybe this apex tanker, tinker mended these walls of limestone, phosphate, and clinker as extended fortress to Sint-Pieter. Like magnetic rocks to the hypnotic flocks, the Emperor's flail had shone day twos tail.

With the absence of Michael, it was mainly up to Elizabeth to figure out these enigmatic ruins. Arthur stayed behind to go through his photos and give morale support to his injured colleague. He listened attentively to the head doctor to get a better understanding of his current condition. Even with modern science, the planet hid away light years of secrets, waiting for the children of humanity, only to reveal more questions than answers.

Her eyes were on the television, the civil unrest was picking up; spreading to the point of becoming the next pandemic. The engraved photo haunted her alongside the nightmares she had, something about the two seemed connected. Michael's discovery even hinted to this, but still no bodies had been found. Centuries of past relics could have been picked clean by some of the locals, destroyed by natural events, or hidden too deep for the current work force to dig out. But, a gut feeling told her that somehow there was a great secret buried amongst those plain looking rocks, strewn apart vines, and echoing tunnels.

One of the men helping her at the site suggested they visit the Akodessawa Fetish Market in Lomé before they left…or before the protests and government began to destabilize the country. She didn't like the thought of venturing alone without her colleagues to hear their observations and knowledge, or color commentary, but, with the current climate, she chose to do it anyway. Hifumi was not fond of this idea at all considering their time limit, and the two argued until he gave in. She had only an hour to be there otherwise her personal escorts, his security personnel, would force her back to the site.

The Market had an abundance of voodoo objects, an inventory putting others to shame. Hifumi also gave her an interpreter since most here did not understand English or spoke it poorly. She browsed through the articles of death: skins and skulls of reptiles, birds, monkeys, even human were present. A local told her stories of how the slaves brought their gods here from Yoruba land and how syncretism caused a great mixing with other religious beliefs such as the saints of Christianity. Soon, she was accosted by an older woman who insisted on selling a strange object to Elizabeth.

The item, an amulet of porcelain with a tulip in the middle, was recently found and brought to the Market. It had several inscriptions on the back, most of it faded. She made out a few words: "Pater", "Sanctus", and several "Est". She and the translator already knew these words were Latin. Elizabeth noticed the authenticity of the markings, as she ran her fingers over it; more jolts came to her mind, but not of the nightmares…something new.

A tranquil feeling eased her headaches. Elizabeth asked if she would barter instead because she had no money on her. The woman agreed, and asked for something of symbolic importance much like the amulet was.

Elizabeth only had one item with any worth hanging from her necklace, her wedding ring. The old woman smiled and agreed to the transaction. She said a few words to Elizabeth and returned to her area. Now the amulet hung from her necklace and the headaches had now ceased.

It was time to depart and as she was leaving, she saw a man ripping open a bat corpse, placing salts inside it. The sight horrified her as she remembered the many corpses with flowers erupting from their little bodies. And just like that, a deep screech that followed the horror show emitted from above the Market. A child pointed to the sky and yelled the word "Ossifrage!" repeatedly, prompting Elizabeth to leave with a mild sweat. The translator returned to Hifumi with a verbal report on her bartered item and reaction to the large bird, more information to deliver to his boss, for she knew much more than Michael and Arthur.

She drank large amounts of juice and water hoping that dehydration was the cause of all this delirium. The matcha would have to wait until she returned to the States.

***

Her return to the Mountain felt like déjà vu; Hughes' ire seemed to have doubled. What began as a simple excavation started to become a military base, since more of his team had gone missing overnight. They questioned the locals extensively, but none had the answers. Some of the laborers began to abandon the site despite the increased offer of pay.

Elizabeth tried to get the story from Hughes but he shrugged her off, telling her to do her job so he could do his, followed by a large spit to the ground.

Her disgust for him grew greater; for what purpose do men feel the need to spit voluntarily, she thought. It made no difference, however, much of the sun burned out from her time in the Market and being alone with E.I.T caused her some anxiety. The challenge of performing under pressure always excited her considering she usually handled it impeccably well but with E.I.T overseeing the project, it almost seemed like they were observing her as part of it. Almost like a firefly trapped in a mason jar with barely any air holes and all alone to be its own flickering light of hope.

Her newly chained pendant gave an extra boost to her light, there were no more eyes peering from the darkness of the entrance. She still requested extra security inside as a precaution, so as not to go through what Michael had dealt with, and as a refusal to die in a dark, clammy, archaic hellhole.

The last remains of the labor force set up streams of lights throughout the ruins, and with a fully trained medical and security staff, she ventured back into the depths of the mountain.

More hours spent on soil samples, more hours spent labeling the slew of vegetation with mottled spots, and still nothing of substance discovered. Elizabeth decided to take a short break sitting against one of the walls. Her glances to the ceiling were occasional, but with how brightly lit the area was nothing but stone could be seen, she sighed in relief that no giant creatures would get the jump on her.

One of the laborers ducked away from his work to urinate in secret. Elizabeth closed her eyes briefly, deciding on a five-minute break to rest. Taking out a small towel, she wiped away a slew of dead skin cells and sweat from her face, pouring cold water onto it to ease her exhaustion from the humidity. She hoped Michael was ok and Arthur was not being too Arthur. She also hoped to find anything at this point before 'She' arrived. An abnormal banging sounded off near her location. This annoyed her; she was just getting her head straight again.

"Hey! Knock off the crap! We're supposed to be gentle with the architecture, not break down the foundation like Turks to the Theodosian Walls!" she yelled out.

The banging remained constant and with a heavy feel to it.

"Why do I bother?" she said, getting up to give whoever it was a mouthful.

Following the steady stream of floodlights, she heard an echo of skittering from above her view. Her eyes, again, did not see anything; tricks of the ruined walls bouncing about. The imprints of his majesty made their way around the bend, making sure not to bring a notice to his camouflage. Its haste to reach the corner before Elizabeth proved true, and the tail shattered all the ceiling lights there.

Show us struggler if these findings are to your liking.
Your occasion to rise is not far off, and we will soon envelope
your troubles. Become my new...

Elizabeth's headaches started again, a familiar voice trying to bore deeper into her mind. A vision of those white cracked eyes jolted across her vision. She thought these words were her own mind from back on the college grounds, but the closer she got to this project...the more she wondered if a psychotherapist was required. The soft echoing voice overcame the amulets blocking effects convincing her she had gone through nothing more than a placebo effect back at the Market. Enough, she thought, someone was responsible for pairing these headaches with the heat and a scolding needed to be dished out.

Finally coming around the corner, she noticed no visibility. Her eyes just caught a glint from the ground before she stepped forward, a fatal mistake of the feet had she progressed onto the shards of glass like caltrops to camels. Was foul play at hand here with one of the nearby villagers? Hughes' team did not seem like the type to let anyone by them, although their numbers were dwindling for unknown reasons.

"Goddammit, is there no quality control to this whole situation? I thought E.I.T was better at handling these types of problems, and here I am babysitting a bunch of newbies. Where the hell is security?"

She scouted the grounds with the flashlight only for her to notice a series of narrow holes, but she did not recall the team beginning the shovel test pits yet. She began to call for them since she had a hunch of someone leaving evidence of their thankless task. From the distance, she heard them coming, but from a few feet she heard something else respond.

The sounds of scrapping nails came from the darkness. A gripping terror seized over her heartbeats again, and this time she was awake. Her shaking hands held the fluorescent torch, hoping her hearing had gone awry. At first, beyond the pits, there was the laborer, in full view, with a large cavity where eyes used to inhibit, receded teeth, and a nose smashed against the rocks.

What followed behind was the thick vegetation moving, accompanied by thin wooden claws.

Erratic murmurs of a low distorted voice reverberated through the tall plants. She slowly walked backwards, hoping no sudden movements would give to chase. Now, thin wooden appendages came to view. How many heartbeats until one of her arms showed hints of an internal attack? Her panic reached the peak. She did not wait to see what else may come from the thick greens and made a run for the entrance. Her screams alerted everyone both inside and out.

Elizabeth made it outside into the goodness of sunlight knowing she was back to safety. Hughes rushed over to assess the situation. She described the glass, holes, and body, but left out the tiny terror fearing they would think she succumbed to delirium from the heat. Everyone inside evacuated and the brilliant lights of a small army illuminated every nook and cranny. They reached the blackout area, but did not see any holes or body, just the broken glass from the lights.

Hughes berated her for wasting his time when he had important issues to deal with. He shut her down for the day and only wanted E.I.T's science department to deal with the discrepancies. How would this look with Michael and Arthur? Even more, how would 'She' respond to this?

Elizabeth made her way back to the hotel, only to receive another scolding from Hifumi.

E.I.T's science team did not make any unusual discoveries except one. They noticed the area, where the body was supposed to be, had thicker vegetation than usual. One went to take samples from the succulent plants and several gushed open with red mucilage pouring out. The ruins had now become E.I.Ts largest priority since its founding.

*****

The cracked earth of barking wails, talons to nails, introducing all to their future jails, would beckon them to the dims of light. Black dug soil was the Emperor's toil, hiding the entrails with pedipalps and tail. A vision, from a thousand long before, hoping none would find the hermetic door. Ancient master of empyrean disaster, waits for the struggler to unveil the gate, soon it shall be for day three has sealed its fate.

Chapter 5: Harbinger

≈

Elizabeth refused to work for the day and decided to switch places with Arthur to stand by Michael. He did not refuse, but considering his background, he felt his photographic contributions would prove to be lackluster in the help department. Elizabeth inflated his ego with fame and prestige what with becoming the first to photograph these ancient ruins; even going so far to say a book deal might happen. He eagerly lunged at the opportunity and agreed to stay out of Hughes' way and assist E.I.T if needed. Elizabeth took this opportunity to confide in Michael about everything: the photograph, the Market, the laborer, and especially, the manifestations from her nightmare.

***

Bright was the day and the heat wave had tamed, but word of the missing laborer from the others moved small groups of the protestors to the Mountain. With spittle, rocks, and miscellaneous debris thrown at the RV, Arthur felt betrayed somehow. This was not what he envisioned his Masters would get him in the future, for although he could not understand the native tongue of the Togolese, he clearly heard the anger from those speaking French, and they would seek an eye for an eye.

Security escorted him to the top, holding back the mob with the help of the government. A discreet expedition turned to a hotbed of problems for E.I.T.

Their power reach had its limits in the small country and the only viable solution was a soft money campaign for a temporary media blackout.

Still, he did not understand why the villagers on the Mountain did not react as their other compatriots. They continued their daily duties, but now they refused to make eye contact. He thought of trying to interact with them afterwards.

Arthur overheard some of the scientists discussing the sudden appearance of *Idolomantis diabolica* to Hughes and it sounded like more confusion to him. What did insects have to do with this project? He would stay out of everyone's way and try to photograph every area of significance.

Inside the ruins, he noticed how well lit the hidden sanctuary looked compared to just a few short days ago when they arrived. Still there were just a few spots they could not attach lights to nor had access to from the crumbling foundation. One wrong move might create a domino effect that could sink everything inside.

He took pictures of the carved words that Michael discovered written in Dutch. It looked jagged and fierce as if bones were used in the process. He thought back on the dinner meeting with Hifumi explaining their initial findings. Collin's name kept coming back to him for some reason along with the initials WIC. Some of the lights flickered above him and burned out. A few of the workers left to have it relit again, and Arthur decided to use his phone as a light source and added a slave flash unit to his camera to provide extra lighting for newer images.

Taking random shots on all the walls, he tried to see if there were more markings waiting for discovery. Browsing through the shots, he did not see anything; however, one caught his eye from the largest wall there. He saw a small shining glint that appeared metallic. Using the light to trace the base, he came upon an archaic piece of silver coinage: a Japanese koban countermarked with the letters VOC. He had never been as ecstatic before since he had never discovered anything from the past on his own, this was his personal treasure.

"How did no one see this?" he exclaimed, going to pick it up.

His retrieval of the coin revealed a huge centipede wriggling about. This caused an obvious freaking out reaction, but it subsided quickly considering he remembered he was still inside a dark cave of rocks and vegetation where things like this seemed common. The centipede's behavior seemed unusual to him, it was not erratic or afraid rather it just studied him briefly. The laborers returned to fix the lights and saw him crouching. One asked what he was doing.

"You'll never believe what I found, and this little horror right here was guarding it!"

While one was fixing the light on a ladder, the other came around to see what had grabbed Arthur's attention. The centipede heard the laborer coming towards it and scurried away to reveal a large severed eye...its pupil constricting to the light. Arthur screamed loudly and fell backwards on the man, as the eye rolled away.

Again, Hughes and his team rushed inside to see what caused the new commotion. Arthur became more hysterical than Elizabeth's encounter with the supposed "dead body" and his words, like hers, made no meaning to Hughes' ears. Arthur pointed where the eye was located and even showed the koban it hid behind with the other creature.

"I don't get why you people were hired at all," Hughes yelled before grabbing the camera, "Useless is what you three are!"

He checked Arthur's photos and noticed something else besides the glint. With the area relit, he crouched down to the floor and noticed a small cracked hole. Pressing his face close to it, he not only felt a strong amount of air, but saw light shining through. Arthur had accidently helped in the discovery of a secret room. Hughes could not believe it, but also seemed relieved because with this discovery, they could now tear down the wall and retrieve whatever contents were inside. And that, he believed, would quickly end this project.

Suddenly, the eye Arthur saw revealed itself fully to Hughes before rolling off again. He jumped back himself, with Arthur asking if he saw it. Hughes denied its existence stating the pressure from the wind became too much for his own eyes to handle.

How would a man of his stature explain this to his employer?

He made the call to Hifumi to have E.I.T bring in people to tear down the wall. He also reluctantly congratulated Arthur on the discovery, telling him his camera was more useful than his peers' own talents. Several of his guards rushed inside and told him more alarming news from the foot of the Mountain where the quarantine tent was. He excused Arthur for the day and sent him off.

The protestors had dispersed before his arrival. The overseeing personnel told Hughes they heard an explosive sound that caused them to run away, but the explosion itself did not come from any human. The puzzled local security searched to find nothing, but E.I.Ts scientists found the cause from inside the tent. The recent discovery from his team had gone missing before its extraction.

Now, planted in its place, were blooming flowers of brilliant colors surrounding a large hole with devil's flower mantes dancing around it.

He wondered again how a man of his stature would explain this to his employer.

***

From incubation to presentation, the forbidden get ready for devastation. Tall limbs and severed pins meet in the close future with none to bring the sutures. With his one eye, they all must die, for soon, there will be a great congregation to start the revelation; release the Emperor and child of mutters for day four has reached its shutter.

***

We stand as numen, for we alone are a part of the amaranthine. The paths of our will ready for fulfillment once more, we release the blind from our agency. Purpose backfired, but it was inevitable from trauma and innocence. Our liberty will bring forth your new flesh, as is our demand.

***

On the fifth day, the riots had finally reached epic proportions across the country and into the borders of Ghana, Benin, and Burkina Faso. Much of E.I.T had already packed up its resources with only Hughes and his security alongside the trio, Hifumi, and the latest arrivals from the company.

Everyone had his or her eyes on the news to watch the chaos ensue. Many were jailed, but some fatalities were being reported. The local military withdrew their forces from the project to bring relief to their fellow comrades. Hughes stayed overnight this time to watch over the site. He hoped he would find the culprit or culprits responsible for his missing members, and hoped especially this would be his last day of employment here. Never one to hide facts from E.I.T, he made an exception to the missing discovery, informing Hifumi of a protestor using a makeshift bomb to do away with it. This pleased him because it removed evidence they were involved with it.

***

Arthur fed Elizabeth all the nasty details he found hiding underneath his new found silver coin. He was extra careful after discovering E.I.T was keeping a closer proximity on them; he had found a micro device in his camera bag, sewed into the lining. This was more reason she did not say anything about the eye to Arthur in regards to her nightmare, god knows what will happen to her if she spoke bluntly.

She might not make it off this continent…

"Ah, before I forget, Michael said he wanted you to meet him by the bar. He's having breakfast there and wanted to discuss something about 'colorful vines.' Know what that means?" Arthur asked.

"…Yeah, I'll see you downstairs soon. Can't wait to see what's behind this false wall," she replied.

Making her way to the establishment, she saw Michael facing towards the entrance, eating his food. She knew things were finally looking up when she noticed his bandaged hand had more movement to it and the color was back in his once wane skin.

Maybe he had more questions regarding everything they witnessed; after all, he took it all in without doubting her visions.

She was relaxed and walked with full composure until she noticed the large chair across from him. A scan of the room showed black suits, with E.I.T pins, watching as she approached, and Hifumi stood by the table now, pulling up a seat for her.

From the oversized luxury chair, a slender arm set down a glass of oaked chardonnay. Elizabeth's spine chilled much like the glass. Stopping short, she slowly walked backwards, hoping to not become ensnared by the slender 'monster.'

Her distance to the entrance was but only a few feet now, but it was too late…

"Come now, Lizzy, I traveled all this way to see you and now you get cold feet? You really know how to hurt a woman's feelings, especially since I put my own money into this one."

A petite Japanese woman rose from the chair in designer clothes that looked business professional. She placed her hands on her hips and cocked her head to the side, looking over Elizabeth's body.

This slender stranger was none other than the 'World of Flowers', Hanayo Uesugi. Obligating her role as heir to Echigoya Industries/Trust, she started as a business owner before becoming a collector for her father's company. He was greatly displeased with it, but nonetheless she still filled the company's coffers largely by enacting a reformed keiretsu with other businesses. Bishamonten frowned on these descendants, refusing to bless them and passing their fate over to Yama.

"Look at you, I can't have my favorite archaeologist running around with cuts and bruises unattended," she said, holding Elizabeth's hands delicately, "Always so brazen, never wanting anyone's help. Let my physician look you over, those 'headache' pills are just dulling the senses for a brief moment in time."

"I'm fine, don't touch me!" she replied pulling back her hands with force.

"I never did anything to you Lizzy. I always helped you out with your financial issues when you could barely keep up with your student loans, the Company gave you sterling references for your career, and I even helped set you up with…"

"Fuck you! I never asked for your help! I never needed a helping hand from anyone, and I sure, as shit did not need you to intervene in my personal affairs! You don't ever quit, do you?"

Elizabeth raised her hand to strike the porcelain princess. This prompted Michael to stand up and tell her to calm her irrational behavior. Hifumi, however, did not move to aid his longtime employer. Hanayo stood still, unmoved as if aware that this was unavoidable.

"You can, if you want to," she said calmly to Elizabeth.

To this day Michael was still unsure why she held such an animosity to the young heir, something about it reminded him of common scenarios similar to unrequited love. On the other hand, there were those who one dislikes for no given reason…possibly an evolutionary defense mechanism.

Elizabeth sucked her teeth and went back to thinking like an adult. Hanayo smiled and grabbed her hand to lead her back to the table. The topic was how to wrap everything up in one day's time. Michael argued it just did not seem possible and they should take their losses. The civil unrest had now interfered with the project and everyone's safety was at great risk. The young heir's face turned from cherub to intense. Arthur suddenly came to join the party without his usual jovial persona; he had been booted from the vehicle until he met his employer.

A meeting over breakfast had become a hostage takeover.

Hanayo rebuked Michael's comment since she placed not only a great deal of money into this personal investment, but E.I.Ts reputation was at a great risk if anyone found out their felonious dealings.

She noted this would be the first and last time projects, like this, get this far in the deep end, but they would finish it no matter the costs. Elizabeth asked why Arthur had joined them when they were all preparing to go back to the Mountain shortly.

"You've all done your part for now, and today will be entirely spent here in the hotel. We can discuss the discovered items, your evaluation of E.I.Ts staff in assistance, and even have a bit of fun later…I have one of the meeting rooms reserved for us to do karaoke in! Don't worry about the wall, Mr. Hughes is guiding some of my latest employees and it won't be long before they have it dismantled like the Amber Room!" Hanayo announced.

Never had the three felt so trapped in their lives. Elizabeth thought back on her nightmare and the supposed dead laborer, thinking they were better alternatives than having to deal with Hanayo. She found out later that Arthur's camera was confiscated by E.I.T for security measures and some of Michael's notes were missing. None of her items had gone missing when she returned after an exhausting long day; the photograph remained on top of her laptop. Crashing onto her bed, she exhaled thinking she would soon return home to deal with her boring job and asinine boss. This put a tiny smile to her weary face. The nightmarish visions would soon end for her.

**

Meanwhile in the twilight hours when all had returned to their rooms, Hanayo was having a drink with Hifumi to discuss darker matters. He told her of Hughes quarantined discovery and how it was destroyed by the protestors. His description of it seemed like something out of a fantastical tale, but she seemed relieved to know of its destruction…too foul for research, it would only bring bad luck. She did have one major request that he performed with stealth…

"Do you have the video ready?" she asked.

He nodded and proceeded to show her a video secretly installed in Elizabeth's room. It showed her crying over the engraved photo in high definition. The video was put on fast forward because all it showed was Elizabeth on the floor having multiple seizures for hours until morning light had finally shone on her face...that was when the screaming started.

"Did you notice when the tears made contact with the strip? A chemical reaction occurred; dispatch the new respirators for everyone in the morning. There is no telling what may be behind this wall. It ends tomorrow..."
He bowed to her and left to make the final preparations, informing Hughes on the current situation. Hanayo sat in the chair looking out to the foreign land with the moon so bright amongst the tinkling stars. She had her own personal photo that never left her person, and stared at it quietly. She with another dear to her, a haiku written on the back from them to her with deepest affection, and now they were dead...never to embrace her ever again.

***

In the distance, the Market had not met the misfortune of civil strife and still resumed its transactions of currency and barter. The child who saw the osprey in the sky met a new creature, with tendrils and nerves. It tried to roll away after witnessing the new power player from the East, to warn the master, but the curious child grabbed it and sealed it in a bag. By stealing it for themselves, they might barter with a loa for their own selfish desire.

***

Bounding main of rich minerals rose once again to flow among rocks, trees, and man. The great glow of perpetual flow, striving to meet those who near defeat sing fallen canaries, the great poison draws close. Beating drums of marching limbs hums the tunes of everlasting grim. Great dog, jail breaks from the masters and orders the Emperor to erect new stones. Poisonous effluvia in the air, day five lost its flare.

Chapter 6: Limbo

≈

$\mathcal{A}$ great wakeup call sounded on the trio's doors from E.I.T, knocks that seemed beastly and wanting. There was no time for food or shower for Hanayo had already received word that the great wall was ready for a single tug to dismantle it. Their exit from the hotel revealed not only their original transport, but also several dozen personal members of her own security driving light utility vehicles; surrounding escort of the RV.

They were amazed by how quickly she had mobilized such a fleet in a short period. No protestors stood in their path and the Mountain, as if fascinated by the young heir, welcomed all without grievance. In actuality, it brought foreign gifts.

The same strange white liquid flowed over the cascade waterfalls and gushed out from the ruins' entrance. Reports came in stating it all flowed from the succulent vegetation. The plants that dried up contorted into wild shapes with incredibly oversized stomata, visible to the naked eye. No one was sure what could have caused this sudden event, and by the ways of causality, the RV hit a large rock that acted as a speed bump causing Elizabeth's amulet to detach from the necklace.

Her headaches returned more forcefully to welcome her back and as a gift, the unknown narrator greeted her with more words and a bleeding ear. The head doctor began to aid her, thinking she knocked her head too forcefully against the side. Her cries of anguish rallied all to calm her. With the vehicle arriving at the base, the doctor was able to apply a cold compress over a sterile dressing to the ruptured ear. Luckily her crystals did not dislodge to cause vertigo, unluckily when brought outside she witnessed a new cause of inner terror.

The natural environment of the Mountain transformed into exotic visions of a remote world. Her vision of the entrance showed a haunting aura surrounding a fantastical skull of limestone and roots, with a spiked antennae acting as a rod to absorb an unknown force.

She tried to explain what her eyes were seeing, but none saw the same. Michael noticed the missing amulet, and dashed back into the RV to retrieve it. Hifumi and Arthur tried to calm her hysterics with the doctor preparing a shot of diazepam.

Witness upon our redoubt; tongues to your mind, writhing about. Long have the tans set, and the crescents rise, we conjoin – tether fare struggler, eons of wait rejoice throughout the enormity of space. Far goes this paradise of burden – your burden. Dash your umbra fears against our pillars; forego alliances, let the inoculation take hold, enter your being and release option. Bask within hermetic alcove, proselyte; cast in your lot. Our music lost to swain drums, transposed to fecund lungs.

The amulet was placed upon her again, and the terrible visage eradicated and all seemed right, or so it seemed, again. None would dare say it, but they knew something was not wrong with Elizabeth, but this completely damned operation. Hanayo ordered the entire company to march on despite the frantic show given, she offered Elizabeth a shoulder; attempting to show her compassion.

Michael and Arthur intervened; they felt the young heir had already done more than enough. With cold water to fill her belly, Elizabeth dared to venture into the Mountain without anyone's assistance, never to show herself as a handicap to her unseen foe of imagination and cryptic messages. With heavy panting, she wanted nothing more now but the ruins to collapse under its own weight.

Now before the entrance, a distribution of galoshes, respirators, and protective eyewear was given to only a select few, those 'lucky' to enter the vastly changing site. The trio looked on with extra caution for this was beyond any person's understanding, but the young heir was resilient and batted no eye. Michael compared the phenomenon to the blue mist of Snoqualmie Falls. No longer was there stability below their feet, terra firma had ceased and small quakes started to occur.

Hanayo ignored Hughes' warnings that the foundation could collapse at any given second, but this only prompted her hunger for what may reside beyond the wall. Now they stood before it, would great riches be claimed or did a vast capacity of nothingness wait for the impatience of a daring princess?

She ordered her subordinates to hand over the remote to induce a progressive collapse so as not to damage its surroundings too much and fall under its own weight. Rubbing the button, an idea came to her.

"End your pain and show your fruition," she said, handing the remote to Elizabeth.

In new hands, the archeologist took hold of something that gave her power now. All stood back to a safe distance with worried looks thinking this was where the cataclysm would find them.

There would be no more nightmares, no more screams – an end to days that came as seasons. The thumb greeted the button with gusto.

The great divide occurred with each rock crumbling down to give a great show of white dust and splashing liquids. Everyone except Elizabeth and Hanayo crouched before the small devastation. New worries grew when the party saw the two sprint ahead into the blinding whiteness, forsaking their own safeties. Hifumi and the others screamed out to them, but no one responded back. The quakes had stopped, and so did the rushing waters. The rest followed behind to see what became of the two, hoping they did not fall into a pit.

"Michael, are you sure we didn't die?" Arthur asked.
"I'm not sure of anything anymore, how did the scans not pick this up?" Michael replied.

Great dull wall turned into a great diamond hall with spiked ceilings imbued with dripping cisterns into a reservoir below. An intersecting bridge of four paths reached to the ends with the two women standing in the round center, unmoving; one astounded, the other...

"Liz, thank God, are you OK?" Arthur shouted across.

She did not reply, but Hanayo produced excited squeals. The party walked to the other sides of the bridge to get a better view of them, but soon they were stunned by what had made Elizabeth speechless.

There it stood, a small statuesque of something in chimeric form. Each feature fighting for dominance. The gaunt cast of sterile mule boasted authority with hippos chest, and marched upon springbok's feet and horns, clasped to the center to gaze outward with calcified eyes. The very question of its provenance would lead to more than just clandestine history.

"It's all mine," Hanayo said, rubbing the disturbing piece.

"Don't touch it!" Elizabeth shouted.

With a bewildered look, Hanayo turned to the archeologist, all seemed right when the statue did not fall apart from the heir's touch; the clasps did not fare well, however, and cracked off the ebon hooves. The dusky manes dull look revitalized with a shine, small veins ruminating throughout the body to expel particles of phosphate. The heir ignored Elizabeth's warnings and reached out again to feel the hair – the animal's gaze turned with full motion to her, eliciting a shriek of the ages from the princess.

Immediately, a gaze of firearms pointed at the breathing statue, Hifumi by his employer's side with a readied barrel and tantō in hand.

Michael and Arthur stood farther away now with Michael bumping into more objects, but not as animated: an archaic book, bundled leaves of a palm tree, and a satchel filled with maps.

Hughes turned his eyes to parts of the walls where unknown shapes melded into the structure, only to notice that one portion was severely cracked and showed the emblem of his security shining through. The heir regained her composure and asked everyone to remain calm and not open fire on the unknown creature. Its eyes turned to stare deeply at Elizabeth – these were the same orbs piercing from the entrance. For her, retreat was in order.

Just like her colleagues, she started to fall back, prompting the animal to start walking towards her, never breaking eye contact.

All of this was a great mistake; there were some things that should remain buried, never to see the light of day. The Chimera pulled back slightly, readying itself to gallop to Elizabeth, but another denied its dash.

"It's mine! I will become the toast of Tokyo with this!" Hanayo shouted with a change in tune, and grabbed hold of the Chimera like a family pet.

The creature stood still to evaluate the one embracing it. Mutual acceptance occurred when it placed its front hooves on her leg. She could not believe this husky thing held no weight to it. Elizabeth begged her to leave it behind, but her pleas still went ignored.

Hughes tried to get a closer look at the walls, but the quakes returned and showed the newcomers they were not welcome with parts of the foundation finally caving. He screamed for all to evacuate immediately.

**

The time of samples and digging had ceased, all had made it outside with their health, but the ruins had now disintegrated – lost forevermore. Michael managed to grab the archaic items without E.I.T noticing, he knew they would take whatever hint of history that would point them towards future safety, without care. In his gut, a nefarious being was present and it resembled what Elizabeth described to him. Prancing in circles, kicking loose soil, disarming of protection, Hanayo rejoiced with the Chimera up above like mother to newborn, a gift from the sun. Elizabeth screamed relentlessly at her, warning this had nothing but signs of an ill fate for everyone.

The young heir brushed her off stating with bold words:

'This is the future!'

Michael placed his hand on Elizabeth's shoulder warning her to stay as far away as possible from Hanayo. He whispered about the hoard he retrieved, this living artifact surely came with a price, but with positive reinforcement, he held the notion the old tome might hold a valuable entry or two. She had no choice but to allow the young heir to run amok with this priceless anomaly.

The Chimera acted so passively towards the young heir's adolescent behavior; there were no nips or struggles to tear away.

Arthur was ordered to take numerous photographs of the Chimera around some destroyed areas and finally one of Hanayo holding it with Hifumi and Hughes present. Out of curiosity, Elizabeth took off the amulet to see if this creature was the source of her nightmares and pain, but refrained; absent were the headaches, the visions, and most importantly, the strange words delivered to her – no need to test fate.

The Chimera stole glances at her; this would be the start of a new epoch once it was revealed to the media, for the title of monsters would see the headlines and new dawn cults would emerge to praise it as a harbinger of some greater deity. For now, the young heir would keep its existence private – a great disappearing act readied for those who may try to spirit it away from the heir's grasp.

***

Jubilee for the penumbra call to destiny, cry aloud the horns to the forest where guardians sleep in the deep. King of the amaurotic bares arms of disjointed bones towards those who must atone. Your time has peaked, now mutterer, Emperor, and marcher must seek. Petals in the totem, surveillance all around, revive opulent visions for seekers of colored emissions. Bring your envoys for eastern deploy, rise mapmaker, show light of the creator. They sought the truth, but it brought no rewards for day six – forbidding, nothing, and nix.

Chapter 7: Advent

≈

E.I.C placed the Chimera in a crate where none could look inside nor scan through. Preparations were made for the return of everyone, but a so-called 'minor' detail was omitted from Elizabeth until now.

"You better be lying to me, so goddamn help you." She snapped at Hanayo.

"I knew you didn't read the contract, but weren't you aware if this should happen?" she replied, looking at Hifumi.

More tiny words she wished she had looked over: *If any artifacts of significant importance were discovered, the acting parties must accompany the employer back to the employer's base of operations for a full broadcast. Tokyo, Japan, the final destination before returning to mundane duties.*

Michael contested the contract stating it only required two of the three members involved. She pointed out that they had no choice since he and Elizabeth were the two.

Arthur sheepishly backed out at the last minute, realizing he was of no use to the project and wanted out. Wide-eyed, Elizabeth showered him with slaps for everything she had gone through, but they were unaware that Hifumi had approached him with a large briefcase if he withdrew at the end. Currency makes almost any human lose their scruples.

He apologized profusely and said he would make it up to her by accompanying her and Michael across seas and try to make it right before they disbanded. His words fell on deaf ears; her fury brought forth red eyes, and veins wanting to bleed blood rather than tears.

***

The remainder of the day was spent packing up to head over to the land of the rising sun. The civil unrest was now at epic proportions much like a virus spreading throughout with no vaccine in sight.

Some of the protestors tried to siege the hotel, but E.I.Ts forces fended them off their temporary fortress.

Elizabeth looked outside her window one last time to see the distant fires hand-in-hand with smoke and saw her empty glass was still on the floor. From quicksilver drippings to molasses, it showed that there were moments in every one's life where none have total control – a spectral design in that everything happens for a reason. No turning back, just one more ride, and soon everything will subside; all to the air and across the lands, the great big show now transcends.

***

Berets scouted the country arresting and smiting any in their way with countrymen and villains put to the cross. Long was the day, but quick was the night, as a nearby village received untold fright. Roaring fires slayed the palms, loud were the yells of battle between two factions – drifter, seeker, mystic creeper, entrance to the light.

There was a shot to the belly with love from soldier to marketer; a new sound bellowed from earth to winds, Ossifrage, bone-breaker, foul of fowls. Soaring above, roaring with glee, he called to his master who cannot see.

Sprouting from the ground the Emperor serpentined amongst the crowds, tail impaled without hesitation, cuticle anointed in splattered gore with reverend sensation. Tackled bodies brought down with behemoth weight, as its poison works to disseminate. Liquid marrow gushed to soil, procured the path of new turmoil; a robed man sent on bedlams accord, pointed jagged finger to the populace before him with one raspy word…

"Oogappel!" he screamed, holding out his hand now.

Terror upon their faces, a cease-fire with legs to stasis, and the enigma marched with a putrid item to lie on the ground. This witness was the stolen quarantine: bog body of the female villager who attempted theft of the living fetish. Patience was lost on the seeker, a small incision to the body to make things bleaker.

Colors arose with mist disposed; efflorescence birthed a new disaster, thirty feet high to serve its master. Angry was the mastodon of garden rainbows – hungry scythes paired with jointed bones. Nervous a soldier became and a shot misfired at the beast giving reason to enjoy its feast.

Rendering the flesh of any in its way, the Emperor joined the noise to uphold its beauteous display. Hooded mystic slammed palms to the ground giving off a drumming so profound. Decapitation became a boring revelation, but the necks had planted for new seeds to grow only to stop when his item would show.

Petite aura came from behind and the hooded seeker withdrew knife from its confine. Quick to turn and eager to slash, a child, no more, would end his task. Detached eye in palms center, he removed the centipede for it to enter. Collected with calm, appendage became balm. Giving visions of those who stole the fetish, now was the time to flee and march over the dreadful sea.

The bone-breaker pecking away and engulfing limbs readied its body to act as transport for its master. He observed its wings and saw more bog bodies encased in stone; it fulfilled its task with Emperor to retrieve reinforcements from the destroyed ruins. More soldiers in disbelief came to fire upon the god of insects. The Emperor injected high amounts of chemicals into the mammoth before it reverted to regular size.

Attached to the back and now new members to the air, the mastodon glowed internally, screaming for its life. With great power came a simulation of the apocalypse and there brew an explosive crater seen from the moon. Nothing existed to prove the existence of monsters that flew silently through the night. A company of irregulars hoping to retrieve the fetish before its intentions made true connection.

Though he could not see their reason, blood feast must enter their season. Emperor must cripple weakest first in order to satiate the master's thirst. Twisted vines to a showroom of destitute morals, prettied with magma dresses and suits, surrounded items they came to loot. Struggler with heir, who was the one they would prepare. Old knives sung with crooked smiles that puked duty, oh how they were vile. Cheers to depravation and the loss of morality, uphold your chalice to show the world their project of malice.

Coming, stowing, and joining the fleet unaware more followed behind and it only took a week.

***

Unbearable, was the keyword running amok within Elizabeth's mind, to share more of her invaluable time with the young heir. She ignored Arthur the entire flight over and secluded herself to the back of the private jet. Michael's plan backfired in keeping the relics a secret; Hifumi was fully aware of his quick hands before the collapse. Threatening to confiscate them for E.I.Ts purposes, Hanayo once again agreed to let them have the works in exchange for copies. He advised her it was not wise, but stopped short when she made him remember he was a tool for the company – do and obey or be thrown away.

Pieces of the puzzle were coming together, all of the discovered maps had WICs insignia on them with only one having VOC. The prize, though, was the old tome, a journal by none other than C. Collins, full name Christopher. Despite the age of the 18th century find, the preservation of words remained largely legible for reading. The others decided to pore over the details of the maps while Elizabeth wanted to read the private entries first before handing them over. Hanayo retreated to her private cabin for rest. She told Elizabeth they should celebrate together in private, and "catch up" whenever she was ready. This was a hard pass from the archeologist, who wanted to delve into the details alone – undisturbed by other facts of old history she wished to keep buried.

She was not the only one who wished to be a part of this. Hughes remained quiet as the others talked and kept a close eye on Elizabeth; keeping track of which page made her face react.

For every sentence consumed would lead to unknown charts of an engraver's history. Each letter branding their marks unto her very being, this Collins was an Englishman, and the parchment showed his descent.

Her fingers holding tight so that no word hid from her view, the beginning unfolded…

Two years out to sea with little to engrave, such difficulties bring more pangs to the heart than the hardship of this quill. Cholera, smallpox, I have seen the sick tragedies consume even the strongest of men. Had I not conveyed from the caravel to my current transport, I fear that I too would have suffered at the hands of typhus, never to see my beloved Aletta again. Surely, devotion towards the teachings of Calvin has saved me compared to those on the side of the Holy See. Though we never saw eye to eye, the ill fate of many Castilians sinks my soul to darkest waters.

Her eyes strained at most of the pages. New entries read – visible for tired travelers.

Contractual settlement for 1,000 guineas just to take the issue was enough to create a comfortable home for us, and another 2,000 upon my return! Dowry secured her hand and I had the parents come with me to my newly owned lands. Hiring a, reluctant, tutor to teach them our words seemed the best choice.

When I first arrived to the port, it became evident of the economic and political stagnation, at least in South Holland – dependence on Crown and Company. The father, respectable, lost all when country turned to memory from close monopoly, putting out hands for charity in hopes town hall would help.

I saw no responsibility towards citizenry that these so-called regents delivered in faith of liberty. He approached me at the steps of my church, in Delfshaven, begging for his wife and daughter's lives. Taking pity on the wretch, I placed currency in hand and bid him farewell before meeting the congregation. The quietness of prayer may have just reached up above for she now stood at the entrance, waiting for me. A wicker basket in hand pampered with small wheels of Edam and brined herring.

Broken verbal connection, her gestures gave gratitude
– struck was my soul. I learned to speak as they spoke and soon
our affection grew. Their lodgings, a deathtrap; no more I
stood to watch such squalor for my home became theirs.
Quaint as may be my duty to her was true.

Elizabeth looked at the picture of the woman she knew
now to be Aletta, how she longed to meet someone who was
just as adoring. Well, there was one, but her sights turned to
another. A moment of weakness forever fouled what may have
been in youth…on to the next entry.

All my lands bought; with fertile soil, a farmhand, and
stock, it became time to depart for the Company. Many hours
spent toiling on the parchment, but success found my talents
once more. A sketched mirror of myself to her and of her to me,
so that we may hold each other close when our minds may
grow close to the wickedness of serpents.
She could not understand why I had to take such a
large offer when she herself was content with what we had. I
implored her it necessary for when the child was born and the
sacrifice of not attending would favor them upon my return. My
child shall not want, and if news of my demise reaches her, I
know that the Great Charter passes my reins of ownership over
to her.
Many maps drawn and distributed to every captain and
navigator I followed. By grace of heaven, it had taken so long
for my legs to reach land again! The sights of Batavia made
this poor man weep for real food and human contact. My
contract now fulfilled, I would depart back home to the lush
scenery of Cornwall.
A man of the Orient noticed my belongings and asked
for an audience. He heard rumors of a new cash crop in the
Dark Continent that could monopolize over many regions.
Before he continued I stopped him short stating I had no
interest in wild chases of myths, England beckoned me as did
my duty to becoming father and husband. His voice continued
to bother, even offering a rare piece of Delft Blue, a single
Viceroy painted center, in my hand along with his Company's
currency of both silver and gold; merchant to Dutch East India
Company from Dejima.

Incessancy bled the ears, and though I declined the generous offers, he handed me a final gift for the child known by his people as karakuri. Drinks were distributed and voices flowed to my bent ear with the acquisition of a wedding gift for my onen hag oll and toy for brood.

Numerous pages in-between felt the hardship of time; too feint to read, what happened here? Her eyes started drying out hoping not to miss a single word that might provide a clue of this strange journey. She had a heavy feeling the further she went into these written passages. The Chimera rattled the cage some on her next reach.

This is the last time I freelance my talents to both of these damnable companies. The director-general has quite the reputation of being a rake, thank above my station was in the commercial centre of the Anes people and not Elmina.

This land is beautiful, but my stomach could not face those imprisoned for sale. I have seen a boy's life cut down when going to escape, just so his mother may receive his severed hand as warning to others. It is hard to retaliate against quasi-governmental powers.

Many days spent under this unforgiving sun trying to map every detail of the land. My walks went further on some days in hopes of finding these vibrant plants to pass on their coordinates to those in the Company who wished to have their identities a secret. The merchant from the East knew from other explorers of these plants, but failed to acquire them or location; tribesman hid amongst the brush, retaliating against fairer skin. Strange little man handed one provision, free, to aid me in this journey: one bird known only as "purifier". Its resemblance was contrary to those of the fowl I have seen run amok in the pens for consumption. When I return home, I must correspond to Linnaeus.

The animal has proven itself an efficient flyer, staying aloft for extended periods. Its keen smell, albeit invaluable, has brought me to ghastly sights of it feasting on fresh carcasses time to time. However, the plants, presumably, release an odor only these creatures can follow.

Annoying, it keeps its own belly satiated while my feet grow sore, and I am unable to take flight to flee from wily beasts of prey – the feline offspring of Nemea's apex have ended many brave men.

Her had rubbed the faded amulet, too convenient for it to be the same, but of all things to find in the Market, a piece of history not of this continent. What other explorers may have lost themselves to cryptic tales to distant lands? The book thinned to the end, something was amiss. The pages started to show splatter formations of dark rusted circles.

All seemed lost, and near I was to giving up all hope; someone has misplaced my compass to navigation and destroyed both sextant and telescope. I write on this beach to prepare for placing the final projections to my design where I am told a massive field lay of them.

The bird finally came across a minute area where some rose…but not of soil, but of the belly of its cousin. Too late, to bring back any as it ate away both red and green. Found I was by a local passing through, and through more broken verbal communication pointed to the small mountain in the distance, where at the peak I shall find my answers.

Treacherous the land, my contact gave instruction to take a frond and tie it with a gold ribbon so that another may lead me directly to these enigmatic greeneries. I should wait with it in the marketplace where they will find me standing by the natives' spiritual symbol known as Ayizan. A loa she is called; spiritual practice of Vodun, something that seems so similar to those of the Holy See's own divinities. I shall enjoy the rest of this day for my own well-being now that it all ends soon.

How I miss my Aletta…

Turning to the next page, her eyes briefly saw the pale eyes of the Chimera; cracking veins like that of painted marbles. Hughes noticed the distress finally, counting the pages it took to get there. She marched onward with each page getting harder to turn for the rusty spattered circles grew large enough to form its own map.

We arrived finally to the peak, but the woman seemed hesitant to speak to me. I heard a voice in my dreams call out to me, soothing, but heavy, a tempest that veered me to another symbol in the market: Sakpata; none spoke of its meaning. As peculiar as it may seem, it told me of greater reward for myself to give onto others. I might be able to help those in bondage.

What is truly peculiar was the passing of a diviner from the south who urged me not to follow my contact. Guards from the company nearly killed the elderly woman for her loud warnings. This "sangoma", they called her, raved with tears in the eyes as if she was watching her brood slaughtered before her. Make no mistake, I felt for her, but to stop now would be a great blunder on my part. I have commissioned some of the company's men to make sure I return safely. We leave shortly; perhaps history might give lectures of my work in the distant future.

The final pages stuck together. Only snippets were legible, but her suspicions were not unfounded. Elizabeth became nauseous, sweat culminating on her scalp – this creature must not follow. Yet, it remained locked, without struggle, on this jet.

Thoughts of annihilation and eclipsed planets appeared before her. What if this was the end? Why would no one listen to her? Her own colleagues seemed more distant; thoughts in tune with otherworldly strangers. She wanted to turn off the mental projector. The only way to get rid of one ill vibe was to counteract it with another illness.

Placing book, and necklace, on chair, she went to the back. Hughes took the opportunity to grab the book. The four men now sunk into a world of ancient taboos. Michael implored Hifumi to have the young heir dispose of the Chimera.

Despite reading the horrific ending, he refused stating she would not hear it, for E.I.T was much more powerful than just a mere cartographer and some pitiful riflemen of the Slavenkust.

"But you just can't ignore this!" Michael said to him.

"A repeat like this is impossible; besides, I firmly believe he was delusional before they bounded him. Violent acts tend to drive the weak into madness. I'm still waiting for a report on the water samples, chances are the flora intermingling with it contains a psychoactive agent."

"How can you be so fucking dense? We are literally transporting something that defies reality! We need to cut our losses and destroy all of this and the walking statue before something inevitable happens!" Arthur yelled out.

"I see you do have a backbone Mr. Dunham, a shame it comes too late after the monetary gift we gave you."

"What's he talking about Art?" Michael asked.

"Oh, Uesugi-san knew Ms. Burke would deny the follow-up portion of the contract. Therefore, we approached the weakest link of you three to buy out. Some friend you are...Arthur."

"You son of a bitch!" Arthur yelled, lunging at him.

The quick scuffle was not without its damage to Arthur. Hifumi had military training, and only the intervention of Hughes stopped everything. He whispered to Arthur to calm himself, a plan was going into motion soon after they landed. The hard-hitting executive exuded a pretentious smile before retiring to the cockpit. His new objective now was to prepare the great reveal to each Chairman associated with E.I.Ts keiretsu.

Chapter 8: Noise

≈

The unusual cast arrived at the prefecture of "Thousand Leaves", a soft welcome for the young heir and her party after many hours in the sky. The darker stage of twilight was several hours away and only a few rested before the landing into Narita International…others caffeinated, daring not to close their eyes if something should go wrong with the special 'cargo.'

Elizabeth emerged from the back, her usual tense shoulders at ease now. Following behind, Hanayo stretched her arms, exhausted yet not caring what others thought of her carefree attitude, power was her greatest asset; through the grapevine, they called her a descendant of Amanozako.

A baggage handler accidently tipped the Chimera's crate, dropping it heavily onto the tarmac. A splintered crack appeared in one corner, and the nose prodded through to smell its new surroundings. Hifumi scolded the man, almost beating him, but the young heir intervened and told the handler not to worry about it and to deal with the other luggage instead.

"That was nice of you. Good thing he didn't notice the snout," Arthur said.

"I will have his job once he and the others are done. I will have to fine him too for the damages; I'm thinking six-figures is a modest amount for an apology," she replied, waving cheerily at the man.

"But he's a handler! They don't make anything like you, have some mercy!" Michael joined.

"When you have your own business Mr. Ferguson you can handle it your way, he should've been more careful."

"Can you just stop acting like a fucking princess when I'm around? Drop the charge on the idiot and let's get this night over with," Elizabeth said.

"…Fine, you're already my guest of honor so I'll be lenient, just for tonight."

"Good, so this dinner thing is our next stop right?" Elizabeth asked.

"Unfortunately, no, it's in our best interest to get checked at our lab not too far from the reveal party – can't risk any anomalies to spread amongst the country. Your health is my top priority now; I heard you went through quite a bit with your headaches and eyes."

Two company cars arrived, and the young heir forced all the men into one, save for Hifumi who rode shotgun in hers, bringing along Elizabeth. A separate truck retrieved the Chimera, none except E.I.T were permitted to enter it, and even Hughes was denied to escort it.

He kept quiet still while Michael and Arthur bickered over the situation; although their friendship was for many years, it was only until now that Michael saw how much of a coward Arthur was. Still, the familiarity did not breed contempt, just pity for the grown man.

They kept asking Hughes questions but he refused to make so much as eye contact through the rear-view mirror. His contempt reached its own peak. If he would become E.I.T's hostage like the trio then his ideas for the coming situation would show eventually. The Chimera situation would become something out of this world's control if revealed.

He had seen the death of men in unforgiving lands while on tour, but this "animal" might be the reason for his missing men, and once confirmed, vengeance will be his, for a stitch in time saves nine.

***

Elizabeth in her own mobile prison looked out to the passing people, the vivid lights, and the clean streets. If only this was a vacation. If only things would go back to normal. If only she never took up the tools of her trade, maybe the nightmares of her current state would revert to just death and taxes. A man in true panic told those final pages, yet still, it did not explain the connection between the Chimera and her fever dream.

Hanayo rambled endlessly about how the party would become the be-all and end-all of her career, Elizabeth tuned her out and withdrew into a nap. Hanayo noticed her sleeping and shrugged it off as jet lag, but the porcelain amulet hanging from her neck caught her attention, and she gently removed it for further inspection.

***

The machination of our inevitable splendor barred, resilience of retainer, unforeseen. Impeccable, precise, just bereft of habitation...our folly. Corrosive behavior returning actions from acts with noise – too animated was the swain. Into the whites and beneath the greys, our oneness never saw juncture.

Our gifts misused only to detain...apprehend...hinder. Behold what you seek, envision our vision.

The blissfulness of sleep ebbs and the vision of bats flow – one cannot ruminate with the council of jargon present, accompanied by close pestilence. Paralyzed body: why do the frigid winds surround the lungs with ease? Arachnid grip tilts the head back; open mouth, swollen tongue connects to excited tiny segments, down the hatch like sword swallower. Now a belly warmer, now a kisser – fiery mandible sinks repeatedly from inside, the smelling of decay subsides. Rejection of stench, it bathes in a leftover pool of acidity and jolts through nasal cavity; segments conjoined to severed nerves – resurrection of optics through Morse code.

Scarred body, angry mind, bounded in this space and time. Great abundance in the torso, anger from another rose from caustic bath, force-fed beforehand. A tempest to rotting flesh clips through the back and straight through the discs, emerging now his royal highness. A growing cyclops to the meat bags back, unimpressed with loathsome company who gushed it into a rotting tomb of petals. The synchronization of meat to Emperor formed an undying bond. Venom animates the meat, the rotted mind retains little knowledge; the nature of animal overcomes sanity.

This beautiful sight stuns the council, revenge for their people with this hideous might! Emperor unbinds impending disaster. The council prostrates to emerging figure, studying the only one to pass its tests. For the others never made it and were thrown into the reservoir. This God of the council was pleased and they rejoiced with loud screams! Dancing around their God, one saw the belongings to the dead meat, began to shred each parchment, and threw the porcelain trinket into the water below. The meat stood quietly until it saw an engraved photo about to join the shred, the councilman soon found himself dead.

Retained knowledge held a great deal to the meat and his Emperor joined in to return the favor. Led astray by their God, the council gone the way of dissection never to see their children and wives freed from foreign rule. All alone was the God, all according to plan for it needed its followers no more.

Speaking clearly into the mind of meat, it dropped to its knees in utter defeat. With a God in its face did it make the mistake of forgetting its place, for Emperor still in motion, secreted new fluids to where it stood; now the God bound in place.

Rising from prostration, the meat retrieved the ceremonial knife used to infiltrate his body. A heavy slice collided through the God's skull, spraying dark juices erratically and partially onto the engraving. Victory went to none for the God's head regenerated instantly – mocking the meat. He screamed in agony until putrid vomit expelled onto the vegetation – the warping of roots deconstructing base properties to bring forth new life of monstrous designs. Strong in creation did this give him a new idea.

Though a lifetime it took, the hidden palace's construct, to jail the God, met completion. Unbeknownst to the meat, he misplaced the picture of the woman during the process. On top of this Mountain resided a King of monsters, striving to stay obscure to keep others away from the God. He takes the eyes of all his victims to assimilate. His mutated creatures aid him for the good of secrecy. Still, he cannot remember who he is...and why that engraving is so important. He is simply bound to the Mountain.

A warm suddenness woke up the struggler, shocking her. They had reached E.I.Ts medical facility, and Elizabeth noticed the amulet in Hanayo's hand. No screaming came with this fever dream, just the fervor of palms.

Hifumi had to break Elizabeth's assault on the young heir, pulling her out of the car forcefully. The others had no idea what was going on, but tried to calm her regardless. She screamed more profanity than usual for what she just witnessed. Hifumi escorted the young heir inside, a dispiriting emotion shown to him.

E.I.Ts guards nearly subdued Elizabeth with their drawn batons, but the young heir ordered she be left alone. Elizabeth tried to explain to Michael that the amulet had a power of its own, and described what she believed happened to Collins after his final entry. Michael tried to explain in a gentle manner that it just wasn't possible to resurrect, or mutate, because of some colorful flora.

"There's a goddamn living statue on the premises, and still you need more proof! I thought you believed me about the visions I had. We don't know its full capabilities, its history, or even if it is part of this fucking planet! Not to mention we don't know if Collins was in the rubble or not!" she yelled at him, "I am starting to think he's still alive out there and he's not going to be too welcoming to us if he knew we helped this bitch integrate this monster into society!"

"Liz, those dreams you had...they're just dreams, much like entoptic phenomena."

"...Are you serious? Did I just waste my time now? Let me tell you something "Mike", but if you believe in the "God" that hung from that cross on your neck, you had better start fucking praying to him now. I doubt the first thing he's going to want to see is a cross."

She berated Arthur and Hughes also before storming inside. Michael asked Hughes for his take on the situation, but he ignored him and also went inside. This neglected feeling of the two men outside started to make them feel like they had no other choice but to be open to all suggestions...no matter how insane it was.

***

Each member was sent to different sections of the facility for extensive testing. The head doctor finalizing over the charts noticed everyone was clean of viral infections or anomalies, save for one.

"What do you mean I have to be quarantined?" Arthur asked.

"Exactly as I mean, we noticed your hands are showing numerous spots under UV light. We need to bring in other experts on the matter," the head doctor replied. "You need to be kept in isolation until we have determined it is safe. Please escort him to the glass room."

E.I.Ts guards approached him with large riot shields and prodded him in the direction of the room. The shouting of Japanese words caused intense fear in him as if he were a prisoner of war. Hearing his cry for help, Elizabeth turned her back to him...another lost, succumbing to betrayal for the sake of his own benefit – the burning bridge set aflame from her side.

"Is this really necessary, he would've walked to the room if told politely!" Michael asked Hifumi.

"Uesugi-san's health above all others, Mr. Dunham's profile suggests he has the potential to run at the first sight of trouble. We cannot allow any compromises; we will make his stay here as comfortable as possible until our team gives me the green light for his release," he replied.

More arguments from the two ensued while Hanayo discreetly pulled in Elizabeth from an adjacent room. Hughes noticed the blinds closed and the young heir locking the door.

Elizabeth prepared another onslaught of verbal abuse, but Hanayo slammed her knees and bowed her head so deeply that it made contact with the tile. She apologized repeatedly for her adolescent behavior. The archeologist was caught off guard by this display, her mind telling her to forgive unless she would become the villain.

She picked up the young heir and noticed the stream running down her snow skin; social distancing retired just for a blink. Hughes noticed from the moving silhouettes that there was an exchange of words, but his attention grew more so when the two shadows drew into one.

"Hughes, I am speaking to you! Get the cars ready, we are leaving now!" Hifumi ordered.

His startled behavior made Hifumi look at him more closely; did he have to make room for one more in isolation? Hughes immediately went to work, taking Michael with him. Hifumi, fully aware of the two, knocked on the locked door gently. Elizabeth jolted out of the room, with her amulet returned, whereas the young heir came outside with a look of neutrality.

"Please be more careful kaichou, as others here might send word to Uesugi-sama about..."
"I heard there is an opening for porter work here, I could always place your resume at the top," she replied, exiting to her car.

He sighed and followed behind. Opening the door to let her in, he heard an unusual noise above him. There, on the ledge of the roof, a turkey vulture peered down, bellowing disturbing noises. Spreading its large wings it flew out of view.

"Hagetaka?"

The caws of crows echoed as well, but remained unseen. His eyes scouted the air some more, yet nothing, and then...abrupt silence. Turning towards the car, he saw the final vision of the sun, its crimson view beating on his face, sending the news – severed bodies of crows dropping onto the cars, the murder met its own grueling end.

Hanayo screamed and ordered they leave immediately; ill omens were taking hold in the corporate world. Security informed Hifumi they would scout the rooftop to see if there were any trespassers. The cars veered off the site, leaving all on the premises to a new guest who brought gifts.

Pristine white, accented with haema, chrysanthemums bulged out of the dead's beaks – choking on stems, wishing to speak: Afoot! Afoot! Our design is its absolution! Grieve no more, for sovereignty declares upon this edifice! Our innards offer a path for liege, ruler, and king, for the Emperor do our mute voices sing!

***

"Is this going to take long?" Arthur cried out from behind the glass wall.

"As long as it takes, I will inform Han-chan when you are good and ready. Best to stay quiet, these tests will be invasive I must warn and will hurt you if met with resistance, much like your fight with Hi-kun. Picking a fight with someone who used to protect the Kokkai's majority party was quite stupid of you," the head doctor replied with an apathetic tone.

***

E.I.Ts security arrived to the rooftop to find nothing amiss. One officer observed a vent ajar, both sides crushed in. He alerted his senior, but no adult could crawl into such a tight space. They would still check the ventilation system regardless. The schematics showed each path was too tight to pass through except one that would lead to the basement.

The march of drones commenced...

***

Her mind nearly shattered at the disgusting sight, Hanayo puked on the sidewalk when Hifumi opened her door. Elizabeth exited the car to approach Hughes now before the young heir regained her senses.

"You need to get rid of that thing! You saw what just happened! Birds don't just drop dead from the sky in scores, dismembered too!"

"Beebe, Arkansas was greeted with roughly two thousand red-winged blackbirds strewn everywhere in 2010 and 2011. Large die offs also occurred in Faenza, Italy and Wales where starlings were found spewing out their organs. There's a logical reason for everything, not some dead Brit come to collect his crusty old maps. His journal doesn't even mention the animal obtained. So, I saw nothing."

"I never took a man like you for being blind, deaf, and fucking dumb." She snapped back.

"...All you do is curse and get too emotional. You put on this tough exterior, but we've all seen you sob into your bottle over some college sweetheart. Your image to portray a strong woman is lacking. You are weak, plain and simple."

Her eyes welled up like before, but she remembered the new piece replacing the old from her neck. Fists shaped from her thin wrists to show what strong meant...but another denied her the pleasure.

A crack to the large man's jaw was well heard round the city. Even Hifumi grinned in pleasure from the sight of his subordinate wiping a touch of red from his mouth. Elizabeth was shocked to see that Michael returned the favor instead. Now he took control of the situation for once and could not stand to see everyone, himself included, look down on her.

Hughes grabbed Michael by the neck and tightened his grip. His veins protruded to reveal his own hidden talents, but sadly, for him, the young heir regained her composure and ordered him to cease the would-be assault. He had forgotten that they were still in public, and now at the foot of the young heir's penthouse. Some passing citizens already had their phones out to record his strength, whispering to each other in fear. He looked at Michael with a deep look of hate, and dropped him to the ground.

Elizabeth helped him up, praising him for acting like a man. Hanayo threw off her soiled blazer, telling everyone to get inside and prepare for the party that would resume in a couple of hours.

"Please…Hanna, get rid of this thing. I'm truly asking you to just listen to me on this!" Elizabeth pleaded.

Now, the young heir slapped Elizabeth.

"After all this time you now dare call me by that name! What next, using old pet names as well? No, you received enough from me as it is with your little photo, bottomless drinks, on-hand medical aid, and even the idiot at the airport! This party is going to happen, it is already prepared, the guests will arrive to the showroom soon, and everyone will praise me finally! This "thing" will not just be some dumb display in a museum for mere pictures, but it will grant E.I.T worldwide influence and as such, I will present it to my father as a gift tonight!" she shrieked, "Kachou, bring the box now!"

Hifumi ordered Hughes to use the service entrance so few eyes could see it, bad enough a skirmish and unhealthy sight of the heir occurred he knew his Company's competition were watching close by – it would be harder to hide bodies at home than in Africa.
The entrance doors finally opened and through it came throngs of hospitality workers from the Company bowing down to welcome back the young heir. Elizabeth and Michael followed behind her, each saw a random eye leering at them from the workers.

"I was hoping you could prepare with me tonight and catch up some more, but I've changed my mind. You and Mr. Ferguson can stay on the lower levels; you will wait for instructions," Hanayo said entering the elevator alone, "Goodbye Elizabeth."
"I'm shocked she actually called you by your full name," Michael said to her.
"…Just shows how pissed she is. Never mind that, we need a plan."

The two went into details of trying to steal the creature away, but they could not come up with anything. How could a couple of experts in natural sciences become skilled in the art of thievery? Michael made a joke about how he, Elizabeth, Arthur, and even Hanayo complimented each other like interdisciplinary disciplines of academia. Her thoughts were too engrossed in the situation and she saw everyone in a view of holism…the Chimera's existence proved that reductionism must be avoided.

Elizabeth did not need another headache and decided to put the TV on in their quarters. Clicking through the channels that she could not comprehend one channel showed enough to know what was going on. All over the news, blazing infernos and covered bodies of all groups and sizes were shown at the Togo Market. The two glued their eyes to the horror thinking they left just at the right time. Michael pointed to one of the covered bodies where the foot resembled his hand during his initial injury.

The unknown stalker they never found in the ruins left a clue on the corpse. Now they wondered if her nightmares were a part of reality to leave the Mountain, in search with their master. Michael hoped the night could end quickly so they could check on Arthur's status.

Elizabeth was unsure what to say to him, but it did not matter. Once the reveal was initiated, there was no telling what course of action history might take. The thought of her own body exhumed from the earth to be set under the microscope by some distant civilization made her search fervently for the amber bottle.

***

To the untrained eye, the lab appeared as a mundane building; short in stature, never attracting unwanted attention. A nature trail, beside it, leading to a small forest, seemed unusually quiet. A young couple hoping to fool around inside stood still by the entrance. The girl kept resisting, but her opposite kept pushing – no eyes will watch us here. Brave Romeo stepped in and turned his back to the forest to show his bravado to the darkness, only to hear the sounds of inarticulate snarls from behind.

The girl screamed and saw a giant centipede crawling over his sneakers; both flew from the scene and from the darkness a mist of colors were expelled from the one who snarled.

***

Arthur paced back and forth in his containment, looking at the clock every few seconds, hoping they found the answers. His pleas for a return of words meant nothing to the desensitized group. His pacing resembled a caged panther, but his sweat said guinea pig.

The head doctor's neutral demeanor diminished with each test showing insufficient evidence of regular abnormality – an infuriating titan demanding results. A skin swab to the mucosa for viral cell culture and identification detected unknown properties. The blood tests results showed the same, her temper was rising. She knew she could not hold him forever, but the young heir promised a large bonus for any new discoveries made – anything to make the Company more powerful for future takeovers.

***

Two bumbling fools from security decided to check the basement, hoping to play hooky while on the payroll. Discussing their gripes with home and work, one decided to mock Arthur's behavior, pretending to be him, gestures and all. Both laughed aloud until the light fixtures turned off, they saw some circuits sparking from the breaker boxes. Groaning, they knew they had to work and went to go see the damage.

***

"Hey, oh what the hell is going on here? Doesn't E.I.T have a backup generator?" Arthur shouted out.

"Please be quiet Mr. Dunham, they will kick in momentarily. This is a no win situation for me, it is impossible to work with this time-limit!" the head doctor replied.

The scientists pulled out their UV lights until the darkness passed. Quick to notice, the doctor saw Arthur's blood react to the UV's. Her eyes excitedly studied the vials that glowed before her; the missing link was in her hands.

***

The two slackers managed to fix the breakers. One had noticed markings on the ground that led to the circuitry, and there they saw something unexplainable. Radioing to their superior about the find, they continued to look around.

***

The superior requested one of the scientists to accompany him to identify the finding. The doctor paid zero attention to the ruckus, deciding to look at the blood via electron microscopy before the power went out again.

Downstairs, the group looked over their finding; the scientist was alarmed by it – a two-foot translucent slough appearing as an arachnid. While they gazed upon it, the main power to everything met a behemoth's mace…a shame they could not see, but feel, their glorious grace.

***

"The leukocytes are diseased, but how can there be a presence of semiochemicals and allelochemicals! This cannot be right…my eyes must be tired. It's as if his body was slowly being used as a vessel for something inside him and acted as a emitter to lure what caused it!"

From fluorescent light to the dark of night, a guest scurried in to exhale its blight. UV candles lighted once more, but the booming of doors hit the floor. Exalted quakes raised the stakes; beams of lights were in all directions, where no answers existed, only questions. They, of science, grew with fear, feeling a presence so close, so near. To the God of Christ, one would pray, anointed on his dome, a show to display.

Blaring trumpets from the depths of his bosom all saw his head meeting erosion. The running of roaches in hazmat suits did each find their mortal loots. Led to the feast, doctor, front row for you – malicious mace forever slew. The walls took up a new coat and the machines stained, taking up the torch to watch helplessly while others were maimed. Invisible force eviscerating with no remorse, where was it, what was it, how could this be! Torch to the ceiling its presence now seen, UV light exposed the being.

Veiled wraith illuminated; the intermingling of greens and blues forging the limelight – molted Emperor reborn as Titan, cyclops retired, and change in the house of prying eyes! None to witness the trepidation of its overgrown bulb, just four eyes synchronizing with troubled lungs...paralyzed.

Pissing venom from the bulb, this predator would study the doctor. Unmoved, unappealing, this was not its meal. Skittering across the dark floor, this predator found the one its body adored. Releasing soundscapes from torturous realms, this predator gave greetings on uplifted legs – the eyes of its victims were pulsing and bulging from between the lines of clunky armor – are you ready Arthur?

"This can't be real...I never got to say sorry!"

Final words from a coward with good intentions, syntax met mutilation, forever gone, conjoined with devastation. Leaping fury through the glass landed on this poor man. He shrilled, he shrieked, his lungs met the peak – cancer setting in. 'It is only a dream', he babbled, these limbs pulled like dough are simply clay, a fever dream, that must be it, just like Liz...I, too, will wake up on a soft floor with all my fluids...assembled, safe, body congruent.

Lights scattered into the room where E.I.Ts security heard the wails, but they were too late – just a fail. Doctor muttered with UV still in hand, and yet the words they could not understand. Rising Emperor appeared to the crowd with wet claws, thirsty eyes, and Arthur's head held up high. Shooting with love, its body fell back from the ongoing slay in an ugly display; crunching appendages, they surely won.

Doctor saw division splitting down the center – myth reborn in this chamber! Ten foot mass reverted to two foot critter. Quicker to run, it escaped through a chute taking advantage of undefended route.

"Parthenogenesis?" she asked herself.

Screams of men filled the halls as they witnessed its actions – friends, acquaintances, no human should end like this. They started to search the grounds, and reinforcements came, but originals who met the Emperor's maim. Superior, egg, and two fools appeared in the lab with mute lungs, unable to speak. Lacerated centers revealed glowing eyes – too late, they could not attend the reveal, but to the passions of a conflagration.

The social scientist taught at the University, and was loved by his peers for his bumbling personality. He translated numerous works even analyzing suicide letters and emergency calls, and dabbled once as a lexicographer, but it was not enough to save him. His call to the Buddha never made mention of horrors like this, meditation still new, and Vipassanā never came through. It was a penance like no other, dismissed from life, forgotten…what a bother.

***

"I am unable to get in contact with the lab, the emergency alert came in," Hifumi said.

"Tonight I want you to forget about it, they can handle one man. Our rivals would not dare use force either; maybe someone overcooked something in the microwave. Watch over my doors until I am ready to leave…I need some time to think before dressing up," Hanayo replied.

"Of course, Kaichou."

"Wait…just this once, check to make sure everything is ok there. Maybe a rival is trying to ruin my party somehow. Be quick, and return to me immediately."

He bowed and left the premises to get an update on the urgent alert. His eyes saw the same vulture perched on a light post across his way; the very being confirmed his suspicions of ill omens. His sights, however, did not notice the slime trail leading to the service entrance.

The young heir stared out the large windows and saw just small glints of the sun disappearing. She decided to make a video call to the one she truly wanted to be a part of the party. Slightly nervous, she waited in front of her computer for them to answer her call.

Repeatedly looking in the mirror to see if her hair appeared prim and complexion looked appealing, the minutes felt like hours going by on a broken clock tower…but they answered the call.

She bowed to the guest on the screen as her servants did with her return. After simple greetings, she asked if he was still attending the party that night. The man must have been born with a look of boredom because his expressions never changed to anything but disinterested. He agreed, but only if she would meet the man he had arranged for her to meet as his plus one. Now she was the one reluctantly agreeing, and soon the call ended. More troubles for the young heir, even Hifumi was unaware of these turn of events.

She still had another hour to get ready, why not reenact Elizabeth's means to remedy by way of the drink. Never turning on the lights, she took a stroll to her room where the Chimera greeted her – freed from its captivity.

"I've never had a pet, do you think I am bad?" she said to it.

It grunted, shaking its head off non-existent fleas. Her hands caressed its head, and the creature decided to walk away to her nightstand, staring at her plant with great interest. Its upper body jumped atop it, and she saw it consume the green as if it was starving.

It tipped the soil over, but instead of anger, her joy increased with the knowledge of what it required. She hurried to find another plant to bring it, but it declined.

"Are you full? Do you even get full?"

It galloped to another area to consume the same plant as before, and then it curled into a ball, closing its eyes to fall asleep.

"My Chinese Dunce Caps, do you prefer those instead? Wait…all the vegetation in the Mountain, succulents. I will give you as much as you desire. Soon, a new Company will rise, and you will stand with me on the new mountain!"

Disrobing down to her birthday suit, she wore her favorite silk robe and headed to the upper level balcony, to get a reprieve from all her troubles. Gazing over her beloved city, she sipped from her glass with many thoughts trying to take advantage of her attention. Alas, only one thing calmed her now and it was the photo of her dead love. Her soft lips mouthed the haiku repeatedly – too late to change the past, now her own karma came for her.

***

Electric wails affected the would-be discreet lab's location. Hifumi could not understand the need for a mass gathering of first responders, civilians, and now the media, until he saw the flames spitting out of the windows.

Only a few officers of E.I.T, left to guard the outside, gave him the story. It was too confusing; they talked of a blackout before an explosion erupted to the front. He concluded it was a rival committing arson.

He avoided the press and investigators; he needed to notify Hanayo of the circumstances. The ringing of alarms disrupted his concentration, and he decided to make the call at the entrance of the trail. Pacing inside, he could not understand why she was not answering her cell; the damn device was always in her hand! His call went straight to voicemail, and he was almost to the point of yelling, when a small trip occurred underneath him.

Upended thick roots protruded from the ground, jutting throughout the trail. A presence was felt, but with the trails lights vandalized, there was only the nature of the moon-streamed visibility…with barely to give. The panting of lungs emerged from the darkness; the doctor had survived the explosion, but her body resembled a survivor of an interrupted ritual. There was a large laceration to her throat, her hands reaching out to Hifumi exposed peeled nails and lost fingers. He rushed to her aid, but the presence he felt was not her, but of another.

It leapt from the trees and trampled him into the ground, pulling his head up towards the doctor. He tried to scream for help nearby, but not only did the droning sounds of the alarms continue, but now his neck felt what he knew severed the doctor's – make a noise and you become the next fish.

Hifumi knew it was a man, but something was off, it was too strong to repel, too quiet to ambush, and now what was happening to the doctor.

Then he spoke, and his prey knew who…or what it was.

"Hi…kun…!" her final words uttered.

"**…Kijken**" the voice said above, with gravel in his throat.

The doctor started to hold her belly, dry coughing violently. The clear fluids of her saliva swapped colors for bright red gore. Her head tilted backwards, blood overflowing from all holes. The man released Hifumi's head and placed his palm to the earth, vibrations occurring, and a control of the wild roots coming together.

Threads of wood intermingled with one another to present untold power – a beast of tusks and lumber. The strange abomination personified the bleakest regions of the oceans, nothing but mouth and body. It went as quick as it came and from under the doctor's feet came consumption with a single bite. Blood trickled down the jaws before releasing, only to reveal the doctor now stood as a deformed tree, roots upending the area.

The ghastly sight caused Hifumi to hyperventilate, in all his years of living this became a rare time for tears to flow down his face. Forcefully turned onto his back, his eyes witnessed a hooded man with nothing to show in the darkness besides a large beard. The sharp blade sheathed back in his sleeve, the stranger held the large shark of timber over Hifumi's head, mouth open, waiting for the command to bite down. The stranger found his next target from the wallet, revealing an E.I.T business card with the name, 'Hanayo Uesugi.'

"Opperhoofd!" he exclaimed.

His hold over Hifumi ceased, the enigma of tongues ordered the beast to open its jaw. There, he walked into the belly of it, using its fantastical might to transport below the earth, melding into the environment, eager to use the ghostly chariot to his purpose.

The bludgeoned section chief knew his sole role was not to the father, but to the protection of the heir. Pinging hushed mouths from his phone, they raced back to her sanctuary, which soon to be defiled. His fingers were growing numb from the redial button she still did not answer, even trying to get in contact with Hughes, who was now reported AWOL after releasing the Chimera. She was not without surveillance, a wandering eye kept watch over her or more so from below – movements recorded her and the resting of the animal, soon to be delivered to the master to conclude this charade.

***

Dropping, undiscovered, from the balcony with no consideration for time or its own safety, it splattered to the ground. Shadows hid the presence of the Emperor, still regenerating; spewing an eye from its torso, absorbing the remnants of the prey to gravity, the transferring of data now a success.

Arriving from the hells of turned soil did the hooded enigma reappear, and his transport broke to ashes, there was loss of power, but it was rejoined with nature. With the eye in his possession, nothing stood against his prowess. Hacking up a flower, he fed it to his wounded servant. Rejuvenation took hold and the King became agile, climbing aboard its usual vessel, ascending to the tops of the building, all ready to greet the princess.

Secrecy is the key, and moonlight revealed too much from the balcony…sometimes attacking at the gate is the only option. Slithering through more chutes, a single sentry stood before her door, and the enigma greeted him with the ugly blindfold. Launching itself down the hatch, his screams were dampened, and the heinous insect burst through the trachea and finally through the sockets before collapsing.

He collected the dismantled pair to feed to his Emperor. Zooming sideways to the stained door would show the great shadow of gods and monsters executing judgment upon royalty, the Emperor scrambling its legs outward, chattering in a disturbing whimsical tune. It was so close, doorknob within reach, but the presence of cracked stone eyes repelled the enigma.

He felt its presence, but with change. He heard it gallop about on the other side wildly, something amiss. The original path was the only way now though he required help.

***

The young heir heard the noises of the awakened animal galloping down below and thought hunger had set in again. Her sights did not see it over the railing, the noises turned from soft to thunderous and she grew fearful. Her descent was halted by the currents growing wildly from outside. She yelped at the sight of her photo blowing about. Her legs reacted faster than ever, but her eyes missed everything.

With the prize in her possession, she came on a silver platter for another, and there she saw a vulture shrieking at her. She stared at it thinking it would attack her, but it flew off. Her phone on the table was lit up with notifications, the messages sent by her second disturbed her, and a soft thud was heard from behind. There she saw him standing on top of the balcony, knife in hand.

His body pounced high above, the strike barely missing the fatality only to crash through the furniture. Her feeble evasion did not go without punishment with the arm sliced, blood-curling screams echoing throughout. She cried out for help, a path of blood left behind and soon her legs started to stumble from the shock, trying so hard not to trip down the stairs. She looked above to see him standing in the center, ready to strike once more without fail.

Hypnosis of terror seized her senses, mouth agape, she of pearls was unable to think rationally —an offering to swine. The pursuit over, he leapt to recreate the scenario of victims who stole in the night. Her final screams emitting to all of Japan.

Heaven did not hear her pleas; that of stolen artifact returned favor. Stampeding obscurity jumped from behind the heir to clash into the stranger mid-flight, his body planted into the wall before the front met the ground. Standing there in amazement before her was the Chimera, its height rivaling Mt. Fuji now. A feel of security overwhelmed her; she grabbed hold of its neck, weeping into the mane.

The crunching of cracks transferred to her ears. Fearing for the worst, the sight of glory turned into broken veins throughout her savior's body. Sadly, in the blink between time and space, the great body shattered into glass then to powder. How she wept some more thinking it had died, only to see from the ashes that it had returned to its original format…staring at her with innocent eyes.

She refused to let it go again, her knees tried to warn her of the cuts they sustained, but she refused to listen to pain. She and this creature were meant for one another, she thought, bound by fate. Nothing but the Devil could separate the two, and the Devil answered.

"Trekpaard? Slecht…SLECHT!" the stranger screamed, trying to get back up.

There was another bellow from the vulture outside, but the stranger dismissed the calls, staggering towards the heir. His Emperor released itself to escape knowing it would live to fight another time. Unable to run, and her savior too small to fend off the attacker, she recited the haiku. With his palm held against her head, he screamed once more before plunging.

"ONHEIL!"

She felt the warm fluids running down her face. Her sockets were covered completely with the mess, and the ears drummed aloud to greet sounds of fireworks. Flashes of memory took hold, would she see her dead love again? She was lost in the past, full of agony, hate, and surprisingly, love. Seen as an infant to lead her Company; there were too many whispers from executives from a safe distance, only handshakes with a smile, prepping the other with a knife once she turned.

She was never one to get along with colleagues –
snakes sweeping through the fields of tall grass. The simple
warmth of another she too thought was meant for each other.
She disregarded the conspirators; this one had all attention she
demanded, so bright, full of smiles, always a pleasure for
company, the best encounter in the same University outside the
homeland.

Tall, ambitious, and at oddest of moments, humorous,
this presence made all the difference; the vast immensity of
space to socialize, let alone become enamored with, offering
company. She permitted them entrance into her room one late
night; they were too drunk to care about time – griping about
recent flame, now extinguished. Never knowing someone so
intimately, she struggled to respond with the same fire
relinquished from her acquaintance's lips…just nods, just
laughs, bent ears.

Crushed cans littered the floor; her colleague's face was
flushed from the pale lager, swishing about inside her, causing
small burps. They staggered to the window and detested their
current situation, but the heir stood adjacent to give slight
comfort, only to become eye-locked. Her guest thinking she
had over stayed her welcome felt the heir take hold of her
hand, and speak of the brevity of human life. The heir's
charismatic words convinced her colleague to stay for the
night; it was a chance to learn from each other…

***

Hanayo opened her eyes, wondering why heaven left
the mess upon her porcelain face. The stranger's body pushed
back with his arms riddled with bullet holes.

"Kaichou!"

Too swept up by the distractions of panic crossing to
levity, she failed to see her second-in-command bursting
through the doors, unleashing cartridges into the daring
intruder before he achieved his goal. Dark fluids ricocheted on
her from his body; warm, but not compatriots of the heart's
vessels.

She rushed to him, sobbing uncontrollably, her words shaken like a child without mother. E.I.T security swarmed the penthouse to secure the premises; some could not believe the abominable sight of their dead coworker. Hifumi consoled the young heir and ordered the men to bring the intruder over.

They crushed his knees and dragged him to their employer, kneeling to his new gods. The young heir noticed Hifumi's body with all its abrasions; she asked how it happened only to be met with a nod towards the stranger as reply. The tears evaporated from their origins as hatred came to the light. She ordered for the removal of the hood.

The intruder's facial features – scarred, stitched, and eyeless, took all aback. He refused to answer their questions, only growling back. E.I.T prepared to call the police, but the young heir intervened, planning something more nefarious for the would-be assassin. Hifumi swore them to silence to prevent a scandal, but the team knew what they signed up for, keeping promise of their oath to the Company; they prepared the body of their fallen brother for future events.

"Have the Goten-kai send their specialist to the 'interrogation' room," she said to him.

"Of course, and I will cancel the party for another date."

"Don't you dare, Elizabeth will never return again, and neither will my father! Send the doctor over to tend to me, it starts soon, I shall casually delay my entrance."

"Kaichou…she is dead…I cannot begin to tell you what has happened to her and to the lab, but that man is too dangerous, I don't think he is even human. This is an emergency, there's always another…"

"Time? I know the brevity of life more than most," she snapped, wiping her face, "I will take these drastic measures into my own hands and I will prepare the dead's arrangements after tonight. Echigoya Industries Trust stands against all who oppose it – the media, our rivals, the Diet, not even this putrid sorry flesh before me can topple my Empire! Keep him alive, I want to deliver the final blow, but first…"

Seizing hold of the craggy blade, she plunged it into the stranger's chest – mad was the smile that ventured her mask.

"Let me deliver the first experience of what awaits you," she finished, phlegm following in kind to his face, "Leave the knife in there until I arrive. I will send our two guests downstairs away now, can't have them becoming suspicious of what is going on. Leave me!"

They used the service entrance a final time and cut off the power to it, thinking that was his original entry inside, unaware of another trail of slime following their transport – leading the others to the master.

Hanayo looked everywhere for the Chimera; its presence was missing. The frantic mind had gone through so much and this creature seemed to reprieve her of all the ongoing traumas. Her guests were all arriving now, that was what mattered most to her. Hellish machinations ruminating through the greys – altered thoughts that mimicked a riddled mind, victim to neurosyphilis.

She discovered it inside her walk-in, eating away the roots of her succulents. Oh how she laughed maniacally knowing this small creature possessed unnatural power, power that protected her. The call was made to a local florist, they did not intend to procure her order so late until she sent the electronic payment – numerous were the zero's.

The stage was set, but the original appeal repelled her; linen of a darker cloth matched her current state.

Chapter 9: Demiurge

≈

Elizabeth and Michael entered the large banquet hall, greeted by the upper crust; the two ignored by the gathering that showed no interest in their backgrounds – it was unsavory to shake hands with dirty nailed occupations.

"I don't see her anywhere," she said to him.
"I thought you were trying to avoid her?"
"I am, but wherever she is, so is that freakish creature."

She noticed more security entering the hall, a battalion lining up the walls. They whispered to each other knowing something was wrong when they were escorted out of the building with an ambulance and men, who dressed like Hifumi, standing outside. Michael pointed out something more unusual in the hall.

"Why are there so many plants in here? Is she trying to set a theme?"
"Who knows what goes through her head, she used to be different when I first met her," she replied, placing her hand under her chin. It was as if she was reminiscing.
"Liz, I try to keep out of these sort of things, but the fact remains you know more about her than I, why do you hate her?"
"…This is between you and me, do not even speak a word of this to Arthur, but it just comes down to our time spent in college. Sometimes no really does mean no, and it turned her into this disturbing stalker. But…it's also my fault too, I went along for the ride and I saw the sun getting closer on Lantern Night. We worked some things out on the jet, in the lab, and I thought I was reaching her, but that damn thing continued to distract her concentration. I don't know, maybe it isn't too late for her to listen to reason."

"I do not want her listening to your poisonous words, you viper," a gruff older man said, approaching the two in a wheelchair, "Cambridge awaited her after her studies at that feminist playground, but you of all people, took that from me."

Michael stood up and bowed to the man, head of E.I.T, and father to the young heir, Yukio Uesugi. Elizabeth sucked her teeth at the sight of him; decrepit skin, beady eyes, liver spots covering his top with white horseshoe hair, and a mustache covering the entire lip – hair that posed as dentures.

"When she returned back to me she had the mind of some addled child, unable to stay focused on the Company. Anthropology? Worthless! I brought a much better suitor for her tonight, and when I have her married to him, maybe she will stop fawning over that nauseating photo and burn it for good. She calls this event her greatest accomplishment; well I intend to reveal mine alongside it." He finished, his assistant wheeling him away.

Elizabeth swung her body back, exhausted with all the drama and told Michael they should go into the kitchen and drink themselves stupid. He always kept himself accountable with drinks, but this time he made the exception to support her fully – damn the consequences.

He tripped slightly on the huge curtain behind them, his eyes trying to look through, but security backed him away. He caught a glimpse of some men wheeling in a covered container. Now he knew where it would all start, telling Elizabeth his hunch about where the reveal would take place. They clinked glasses and prayed that something would turn in their favor.

The doors to the hall opened revealing the young heir, and her new look. Everyone bowed to her, but the surprise of her new transformation had them talking to each other more fervently. The women gazed at her in astonishment while the men stood silent, feeling emasculated that their female counterparts ignored them. She approached and bowed to her father.

"How androgynous, now I know what my son would have looked like," he said to her.

"Otōsan," she replied in a doting manner.

"Hmph! Good, I grow tired of this horrendous language."

Their discussion went on at length about her actions in Africa; he berated her for misusing the Company's money. He did see an unseen benefit in the civil unrest, taking quick advantage to monopolize on the natural resources, enforcing exclusive dealings to different wholesalers – it would be more money in E.I.Ts pocket to cover his daughters spending and drive out any competition.

He snorted at her look, impressed by how sharp she looked in a man's suit, unimpressed by her slicked back hairstyle. Their talk now turned to his chosen suitor for her, so dull and plain looking, his face as sour as her father's did. When the words of marriage were brought up, her eyes could not see straight – was this how the chapter ends? She dismissed herself to go behind the large curtain, lifting the dark drape of the container to see her pet.

"Do you think I am capable of killing not one, but three men in the same night?" she said to it, feeding it some of the plants. "I think that madman is the perfect initiation for me into this cutthroat world, and once I have him cut into pieces…I will enjoy dissecting my father and that bland parasite he brought along. I will get what I want, speaking of which…"

She asked her guards where Elizabeth was, and they pointed to the kitchen. Her feet headed towards it, but she soon found herself surrounded by many Chairmen of other Companies, vying for her attention. She saw her father leave the hall with pipe in hand; it seemed like a chance to incorporate new deals for her future takeover, Elizabeth could wait.

***

Deep underground, buried under thick cement, the stranger was constrained with chains to his wrists, holding him up where feet could not touch the chiseled floor. Hifumi watched him with two guards, waiting patiently for one to start the process.

Gentle knocks sounded on the heavy steel door. He bowed to his guest, an emaciated man in thick framed glasses, tweed suit, and green turtleneck wheeling in a hard-shelled luggage case. He was excited to hear from Hifumi, asking if he ever thought of rejoining the Akamine family again. He politely declined the offer, his new station to the heir more suitable than his previous works with the Ninkyō Dantai.

His guest laughed and decided to get to work. Hifumi briefed him to stay cautious at all times with the stranger. The man ordered for the removal of his rotting robe. Each man gasped at the stranger's body, and the torturer asked Hifumi if this was necessary, it seemed someone else had beaten him to the punch. Studying the torso's most distinguished marks, he made mention of the cardinal lines resembling Hifumi's trademark used on past subjects.

The torturer opened his case – instruments of death that Shirō Ishii and his 731 would envy.

He started slow with large needles inserted beneath the fingernails, but the stranger did not utter a sound, only keeping his eyes closed. Hifumi stared while his men looked away as the stranger's pit had heated prods strapped on. Stainless steel thumbscrews made easy work on his fingers and toes, but still nothing except closed eyes.

He twisted the knife the young heir planted to try to elicit a groan, yet nothing. Reaching into his case, he pulled out a large choking pear, ready to jam it down the throat with all its miniature spikes. Viciously pulling his eyelids open, exposing the nothingness and showing the empty sockets, the next thing was to greet his insides with a crazed smile, but the stranger returned a smile back.

The soldier of countless legs ejected from one socket, biting indiscriminately, and wrapping itself around his head. Hifumi rushed to aid him, but part of the ceiling fell on him, the Emperor had dug its way down. His men lifted him up and shot at the ceiling, the haunt of the scorpion fleeing.

The torturer managed to get the centipede off him, blood spilling from his gaunt cheeks, lunging at the stranger.

The shortcoming of his attack met with sharp wooden fingers bursting from the stranger's torso, delivering the mortal blow into his heart before pulling its arm back inside.

With the torturer's body collapsing, Hifumi and his men now became exposed to colorful gases emitting from the stranger's torn cavity. The Emperor returned to break his master's bondage. The stranger rushed towards Hifumi, thrusting his entire body into him, flinging his entire body out of the door, and locking it – by this time, the second-in-command was unconscious.

The stranger watched the two guards screaming in despair. More gases filled inside the small room. There he saw the self-mutilation of their faces and the meeting of jaws to necks, finding their deaths consummated by an effusion of gore – anemic animas to the toasting of ancestral chalices.

Collapsing on his back, his movements slowed, the supine stranger reached total disability of functions. The centipede quickly acted as a healer, threading all the lesions back in place – the noxious emissions withheld once more inside the torso.

With the return of his senses again, he stood upright as though nothing had happened. His blindfold retrieved new eyes for the Emperor, saving one for the Master, visions of the banquet hall appeared where he would depart. Climbing through to the top, he saw his flying scout waiting. He transferred the vision of the hall to it and watched it fly to its destination to encircle overhead, marking the location.

Visions of the Chimera streamed in his broken mind – producing rage. Standing atop to stare at the great electric works of Tokyo, he embarked, conceiving a new plan without revealing his identity. If it came down to tearing his own chest open again, self-sacrifice might be the only option, leaving his loyal servants to their own devices.

***

Michael had given up on drink, beaten by his cohort's liver. All of the cooks left for the hall with some brushing past the one with cold eyes.

The presence of Hughes re-emerged back onto the scene, smacking the glass out of Elizabeth's hand, and tossing an ice-cold bucket of water over her. His hand covered her mouth before her usual fury sounded off to alert the guards.

There was no time to waste; his was the final plan to come to fruition – now there was a trinity of perplexing strategies vying against each other. He did not require, but ordered the duo to reach the state of sobriety, informing them of the awful fate of the workers in the lab, and Arthur's.

Michael dropped his hands to the prep table; Elizabeth began to break down with him, blaming herself for not saying proper goodbyes. Hughes shook her, trying to get a handle on the crisis. A car awaited them out back which they would use to flee to another airport nearby, not influenced by E.I.T, killing the Chimera en route.

**

However, the first plan to come into play hid in the vent above the living fetish.

Drool sloughed through the grate, absorbed into succulents, spreading the disease of fate. Wild vines twisted and churned ever so slow they began to glow. The heir announced the great reveal to all, none aware of what was behind the curtain, grand and tall, hidden stems seeking to entwine all portals, sealing the fate of all mortals. Gathered to the front, an excited assembly, the great reveal exposed – a jungle of jades, spikes, and teeth posed.

Alacrity inherited a pillar of vines, cascading into the gathering, and the gouging of bodies rained throughout the hall. There was the trampling of bodies trying to open the doors, none got close, and some were pulled into the sky – torn asunder by the great roots. The master made his entrance from the vent to release his Emperor to aid the violent flora. Hanayo was stunned to see guards and guests split at the seams, vines skewing intestines, some spewing from the mouths that entered anuses.

Aristocracy was unmade through the befouled violence of nature.

She saw the stranger erecting a throne and with great force plunged into his chest, tossing his puppet to the floor. Offering his insides of strange flowers, a circle surrounded it, now enflaming them. Bouncing bent knees and wriggling palms to the sky, she saw visions of dancing priests from his strange pose. The small puppet rose into the air, size amplifying amongst the blue flames – splitting wood forming a face, wailing to the world, advancing to shred all beating hearts within its vicinity.

Through its carelessness, the Chimera's cage toppled towards the kitchen. Hughes fought off some of the smaller vines, while the duo grabbed the living statue, stopping short to watch the horror surrounding them before retreating to the car, unaware of a rogue eye watching them from the corner.

The master sat on his living throne while his blindfold stitched him up again, with the young heir trying to find any exit. She saw Elizabeth and the others stealing the Chimera, but the path was closed off by toppling bodies and sprawling vegetation. Her cries for help never reached their ears and soon they disappeared through the kitchen. Some of the corpses rose as green sludge, pouncing onto the living to melt through their flesh.

A pile collapsed to expose a closet, which was her only reprieve in which she hoped to hide from the bloody pandemonium. Her hands covering her mouth to muteness, her dripping eyes witnessing the ensuing death through the thin slits, the recital of the haiku in her mind, could not keep the monsters away. The puppet barged its head through the bottom, grabbing her legs and the Emperor tore down the frame. Wild were her kicks and screams, slithering vines entered to grab hold of her arms, pulling her up into the air, granting audience to the stranger.

He stood up with the puppet crawling onto his back, and stared at the helpless heir. The wailing child of wood placed severed eyes into its sockets, the sounds changing to rasps. It pointed at her, and spoke:

"The herring hangs by its own gills, give us the horned one, or we will cast the die!"

Terror struck as she pointed to the still covered cage, knowing the Chimera was gone. She hoped this gave enough time for the others to run far away.

"I said goodbye to you in anger, maybe you will say hello to me when we meet again. So happy you were my first...my last...this limerence is reserved for you..." Hanayo said, her head hanging low.

The stranger walked over and unveiled the empty cage, high-pitched roars were emitted, and the great vines ate the young heir's flesh, leaving nothing behind but her skeletal remains. Her shredded pants broke off with the rest of her lower half, exposing her real treasure: a photograph of Elizabeth having her arms around Hanayo, back in college, with Elizabeth's handwriting on the back –

We may be apart
Our paths take us to new worlds
Desire, you, my light

***

He flailed his body, screaming uncontrollably, the frustration mounting. A banging sound was heard from the main entrance, a force of E.I.Ts men barging in with Yukio standing there, bearing witness to the massacre of littered corpses – a final command from the stranger came to play.

Screaming and pointing at them, the large vines lunged to grab each man standing, bringing them to the center of the room, segregating flesh from bone in a tornado of rage. Alarms ringing, water sprinkling, the vines flooded the pipes to block the passages. The nomadic eye presenting itself to the master, and entering its new abode, he witnessed the ones that had caused his entire scheme to backfire...and they were still close. The Emperor injected countless bodies, a grand sendoff prepared.

The newly made trio made haste to the car, Hughes pulling his keys out, only for an unknown force to knock them away.

Ungodly figures surrounded the car, masses of oil breaking it down, and faceless sights turning to them. Monstrosities of amoeba variations, stumbling in unison, muttered in gibberish with the one near Hughes exposing an under layer – unsolved mysteries brought in the revelation.

"Jesus fuck what now?!" Elizabeth screamed.

"…My missing men," Hughes replied, shooting at them.

Fortunately, they succumbed to the bullets, their bodies disintegrating into opaque pools. He made short work of them, reaching for the keys, with a bullet hitting near its location. Behind them they saw another foe, but of the living.

"You…all of you…are responsible for their deaths!" the voice cried out.

With distressed clothes, bloody skin, dragging a large katana in one hand, and pistol in the other – it was the return of Hifumi.

The once calm man was met with madness. He hacked up enough vitals to fill a syrup jar, and spat a broken tooth to the ground.

"She is dead because of you! You filled her head with nonsense!" he said, now pointing at Elizabeth, "I will make you all suffer, I will kill these 'things' before they get to you, your heads belong to me now!"

An enormous explosion erupted from the building practically tilting it to one side. His very being unwavering to the sheer force, the silhouette of his figure in front of the flames continued to get closer to them, gun still pointing and sword slowly rising. He twisted it sideways to show its clean reflection of them, and of others.

"What the hell is that thing, hey man, if I were you I'd turn quick!" Hughes shouted.

"Lies, only lies! In Echigoya…I trust!"

With his sword raised, he felt what seemed like a small child crawl on his back, plunging its arms through his chest. It wailed heavily into his ears as he collapsed to his knees, coughing everything within. Somehow, he managed to use every living fiber to toss the living puppet away, reaching the feet of additional aid.

There they were in glorious poses ready to march their sickness unto the trio.

"What now? Who the hell is this sick fuck?" Hughes asked.

"…It's Collins," Elizabeth replied.

"The dead man from the journal, it's just not possible!" Michael shouted.

They saw more of Hughes' old team coming from the sewers, struggling to eat away at the party. With nothing left in his gun, he attempted to get the car started; Michael and Elizabeth tried to get the Chimera inside.

Though it made no innate sounds, it thrashed about wildly, kicking relentlessly, and biting Michael's fingers.

Collins walked calmly to them until shots pierced his body, Hifumi still lingered behind. With the colorful toxins leaving his body, he breathed them into Hifumi's mouth, his eyes turning red – seeing the true reality Collins gave forth.

"Vaarwel krijgsman," Collins rasped to him.

The car managed to escape, tearing past fire trucks, evading police patrols, hoping to make it to Haneda Airport – with one less passenger.

Collins summoned his vulture to eat the ever-growing flowers inside him, its small body changing from New World to an oversized Old World bird of prey, all ready for the skies once more.

Hifumi watched in horror the switching of reality to hallucination as they took flight, failing to realize the dead men going for him now. They splashed their bodies onto him, incinerating the flesh, with no bones left behind. He slashed with his last bit of strength before they mobbed him – a giant mass formed on him, only to burst into flames.

***

Inside the car, Michael held the wild animal in place while Elizabeth tried to kill it with Hughes' knife – dark arterial fluid sprayed, but they watched as regeneration quickly occurred. Its eyes started to crack, shining brightly to blind them. They had to kill this thing and dispose its body before reaching the airport, or dawn would be a thing of the past.

He quickly steered the car to a nearby park, only it got there quicker, with Collins making the great vulture smash into the side of the car, flipping it hundreds of feet into the most wooded area.

Hughes barely got through the broken window, trying to get the others out, wondering if they were alive. Tearing off the damaged backdoor, he noticed the Chimera was missing. He cursed the world for this nightmare.

Elizabeth crawled out, her body unscathed somehow compared to Michael who was locked into a coma, a major dent to his entire side. They gently pulled him out before reassessing the situation, but how could they she asked him. A giant bird of prehistoric size descended onto them, piloted by a blinded voodoo man of English descent. How could this not get any stranger?

"Where are we, are we far from the terminal!" Elizabeth asked, looking around in the barely lit area.

"Nagisa forest I'm betting, there's no way we can walk there without an issue it's over an hour away on foot! Why don't you ask a real question, like where in god's name is that fucking goat thing?"

"Who cares anymore, we need to get Michael help before Collins find us!"

She tried waking him up, but he showed no hints of responding. Hughes picked him up and they started to walk towards the city lights. Not too far into their walk, the car combusted, turning itself into both bonfire and beacon. The pair looked back at the immense display of autumn colors dancing with clouds of smoke.

"I need a goddamn pint, or four, when this is all over," Hughes said.

"I'll join you," Elizabeth replied.

Skittering through the darkness, another ambush commenced, knocking Hughes into the distance. The Emperor seized the moment to divide them and attack Hughes, leaving Elizabeth in the company of Collins. Landing on her side, she felt the intense pumps of her heart beating against her breast trying to escape from its ribbed prison, trying to take flight from a fate worse than baptism in fire. Some yards away stood Collins, his knife in hand.

The war drums of human versus arachnid commenced – a wrestle of Atlas against Serket's servant. The stinger convulsed rapidly with its strange brew spewing, trying to impregnate Hughes; body. His large size could not evade its rapid movements and lacerations grew in size on him.

He reached for his gun to reload with just one clip, but fate found him with the tail thrusting through his stomach, lifting him up in the air now, and injecting its flammable concoction.

Hughes had lost, but he did not give the Emperor the final satisfaction. Unloading his clip into its legs, and through its eyes, it could not regenerate a new body in time. He gripped its enormous tail in place as it tried to escape his glowing body.

"At the end of the song…it comes down to payment…," he said his last words as told to him by his Welsh father.

With his body glowing brightly, Hughes went out with a bang, taking the Emperor down with him – with nothing to show except a crater with a human shadow etched in stone.

Elizabeth and Collins looked at the explosion, his mind distracted to see his warrior gone. She took advantage to crawl backwards from him, gaining momentum, until something sliced her hand from the grass. Her painful yelps brought his attention back to her and he withdrew a flower from his throat to place inside his now small inanimate puppet, to revive it again.

A rock flew across the air to hit Collins' head, drawing away his attention – it was Michael, barely alive, praying he could buy Elizabeth time to escape. Irritated scowl of blind horror crossed his face as he dug his nails into Michael's neck, tossing him beside Elizabeth to show he was nothing more but a mere ragdoll.

The dripping blood of her hand found its aggressor, Hughes' knife, and she held it up to Collins – confidence overcoming her threats. Then his broken nails finally dug into her neck to uproot her from the ground.

The fears of all her nightmares coming true, the dynamics of everything set into motion just to get away from a bad experience only to set an unfavorable metamorphosis; there was a last regret to not think things through. Collins traced the knife against her face, screaming violently, ready to dissect her eyes to lead him to the living fetish.

There he saw the glint of it dangling from her neck – a name uttered.

"**Aletta,**" he muttered, staring at her amulet.
"Liz…NOW!" Michael shouted.

Time slowed down to a crawl, she sliced the centipede in half, and finished by dragging the heavy weapon down his giant scar – a great gust of colored gases blowing at the duo.

Collins dropped Elizabeth, but the surprise of the strange mists filled hers and Michael's lungs; blurs were setting in, colored vapors twirled about, notes of rotten fruit invaded the senses, it was an invitation to laugh amongst the executives.

With furniture dropping from the sky, and the shackling of chains crashing about, Elizabeth found herself in complete bondage to a petrified seat. There was a center table, but not without guests, for they surrounded it – faces full of glee, clothes of past opulence, and a grand pig served on top.

She watched in despair their gluttony gouge, pilfer, and purloin into its flesh. She witnessed their toasting to each other on the fine plump meal, drowning themselves with wines, beaming at her with such gusto, and shaking their heads in a violent haze.

Aristocratic pigs dined in such a fine hall of antiquity, relinquishing their humanity – how could they cannibalize the pig that was Michael down to his offal?

He appeared at the head of the table, and her own insides tried to excrete with his leering gaze, raising his mighty chalice to the sky.

There in clean clothes without his latest image was Collins, before his vivisection came to be, and from the shadows emerged slaves, each behind blue-blooded beings.

With the ascension of chalices to his lovely cannibals – heads turned to Elizabeth. A wave of subdivisions, crude knives carved their necks, almost a feast for beheadings; Collins cheered the sights of the newly slain. She wailed, but he smiled with his servants, and spilled the contents of his chalice over Michael's body.

His remains wrought screams of a new change for her – teeth sharpening, nails growing, a carcass not of peat and sphagnum, but of wisdom and dangerous hidden knowledge.

Her shackled body tried with all its soul to break free, as Michael grew larger in size, his visage becoming horrid. Skin peeled with each chance of resistance, dangling about, showing the fillet of humans to be no different from pork. Her persistence seemed futile, it seemed best to give up, but she managed, but not without its damage.

She saw a door at the end, and quickly limped in its direction. Michael had transformed into another behemoth of extended limbs and crooked bones. He advanced for the struggler, and now he had an insatiable hunger. With each lumbering step breaking into the floor, Collins watched from afar, laughing at her trying to get the chamber door open before finding herself inside her colleague's bloated torso.

Back and forth, push pull; the stubborn frame would not budge! Overshadowed, she could smell his pestilent odor inches from her. Raising his thorny arm, she pushed once more, bumbling inside, and quickly closing it.

This was not sanctuary, just another trap! The midnight color of blue was all around; there were strapped bodies to the walls, and black oil bubbling at her feet. The oil weighed down each step, almost to the point of quicksand, yet there was another door ahead – forward dear struggler if you want to live.

Foul bubbles popped in large quantities from behind. With one glance, she saw Michael emerging from the oil, snarling at her. Sweat poured from her brow, and fire filled her lungs from the exhausting exercise of getting to a door that was just inches from her – Michael tried to lunge an arm at her, and missed.

Her entry into the next room proved it was the last, no more doors, no monsters, just a golden hall with large steps to a throne, where Collins stood. She screamed not in terror, but in anger. They all died, and she was the last, dangerous was the human that was without any to call their own. She wanted out of the game he played with her, the id eroding from his power of fevered nightmares. Her steps becoming heavy, stampeding to his space, he toasted her.

Quakes snapped apart the hall, and steps collapsed under her weight; she ignored it all, her mind set to kill this pretentious man. He tried smacking her with the chalice, but pulled back at the last second, he wanted this. She pushed him into the wall and saw a knife dangling from his belt, quickly equipping it. There was a roar of roars from her, and she once again dragged the knife down his chest – no gases or flowers expelled this time, just blood.

The split of hallucination and reality finally severed from each other with the stage of blurs setting in, a return to the start. Back to the real, a return to normal. Grunts traveled close to her position, and there, she saw Collins limping away with gases polluting the air. He turned to her with an opening to his torso, nothing, but the flowers he had searched for inside him. Without the marching blindfold, he could not repair himself, and the dead of weight took hold, dragging him down into the adjacent canal.

His body descended into the deep with only one soldier, and without a forced feed of the flora, proved to be nothing more than a tinker toy. Some of the flowers rose to the surface, slightly lit, and traveled down the calm waters – a new lantern parade for the struggler's eyes only.

The nightmare was finally over…

Chapter 10: Seminal

≈

Weeks had gone by, with the destruction of E.I.T and all her colleagues in freak accidents, all fingers pointed to Elizabeth, the sole survivor. Interrogations took place from all angles of the world – a belt of litigations from Japan, Togo, down to the US, no one was the winner in the end.

When the Metropolitan Police found her, they immediately assumed she was responsible for the carnage: the knife was still in her hand, Michael's body had lacerations down his midsection, and she was the closest of the group to Hanayo. They imagined she had worked for a rival company to commit terrorist acts against E.I.T, taking down the lab and the most important figures at the banquet hall. She pleaded for evidence to reveal itself, possibly from security cameras to show them what really happened. There were quick shadows on the data of every CCTV they reviewed, before it turned to static.

The more she talked, the more they saw her as a victim of shock – locking her into a psyche ward until her government intervened. The 'gatekeepers of life' watched her every day without missing a beat until help arrived. With insufficient evidence to prove she had committed criminal activity, she was released and given a one-way ticket back to the University.

Memorial placards commemorating Michael and Arthur were exhibited at their respective colleges; Bryn Mawr dedicated newly planted trees in their honor.

Elizabeth assumed more fingers would point at her on the campus, even thinking her job was gone, but instead, all of her students brought bouquets, cards, and tears to her – they knew she had gone to hell and back, the warmth of their hugs healing her fragile mind.

The Director summoned her to their office, a new tone of dialogue presented.

"I've been keeping a close eye on the news on what happened, we all have,"

Elizabeth kept quiet, her pronounced attitude nonexistent.

"I want you to know, that, I am truly sorry you had to go through what you did...it's unreal, and I will sorely miss Michael and Arthur, I've known them for quite some time, and considering what you have witnessed, I have decided to postpone your courses for the next month. Think of it as a 'Federal Emergency Paid Leave', no furlough, but 100%, just to clear your head and grieve properly."

"Ok..." she replied somberly.

"I am going to send you off with some pamphlets for additional help, should you want it, and here are some emergency numbers you can reach in case you need someone to talk to," he said handing them over.

Elizabeth got up to make her exit; she was going home...where all tributes to suffering can expose themselves to relinquish as the heart aches in peace.

"Oh, before you go, the police sent over your belongings from Ms. Uesugi's residential building. They almost took the artifacts away as evidence, but I told them they were just well made replicas, no need for any more trouble, right? When you return maybe you can indulge me on the book and maps; that's a rare find."

She grabbed her case, and thought of the artifacts briefly, she could not go home until she satisfied a superstition.

When she was still a student, her grades had started to dip, leading her down the path of alcoholism. Thoughts of not graduating at first did not sound so bad, but after Lantern Night with the young heir, she wanted to rectify her current standing.

Elizabeth admired Hanayo's confidence, but her pursuit into Elizabeth's deepest personal moments had caused the intense hate. Had she never pursued her with that aspect, she could have anything she wanted, who knows? Now, Elizabeth wished her phone would light up with her number to hear her incessant badgering – you never know what you have until it is gone.

There in the Great Hall stood the statue of Athena, she stared at it quietly in great length. With a deep sigh, she removed the amulet from her neck, placing it around the statues as an offering to her fallen companions. This was her only way of making amends.

Now, she was home bound.

Epilogue

It took hours to settle into her house, the silence was maddening. Turning on music, she decided to re-read Collins final entry again aloud – realizing what happened to him with absolute clarity now.

The hastily scribbled font was written in blood.

The men, they are all dead! How could I be such a fool to go on this deceitful errand! The voice I heard could not have come from human tongues, but of devils. Sakpata, the one to inflict disease into the mind, it had to have come from him or his minions that ambushed us inside! What sorcery do they hide in this Peak?

These 'priests' keep performing the same ritual with each man tied to the post, and still they are not satisfied. Emptying out their bowels, they stuff the strange flowers hidden here inside their bellies and place a large scorpion inside – only to take the eyes as a personal reward.

The creature grows, and attempts to place itself onto the back of the body, hoping it moves before its shells break to unveil its original size again. They killed several of these things, forcing them to eat the flora, but it appears there is a limit to this taboo.

They come for me now, the last of us, I have secured my love's letter within. Farewell to this fool, for my existence awaits the gates…

Elizabeth flipped throughout the book and never found the letter. Maybe Collins kept it on him, or it was destroyed in the ruins, she thought. She sighed again wondering about the written contents, rubbing her fingers against the backstitching.

Her fingernail accidently unraveled part of it, revealing he hid it beneath the original material. Her eyes grew wide, and with frantic haste she tore through the stitching to retrieve what would seem like a Christmas gift.

Gently unfolding the parchment, she saw the delicate handwriting knowing full aware who inscribed on it. With her mind racing, she leapt to her computer to scan it for the best translation available.

The blue screen slowly revealed everything, and with her teeth biting into her nails as she waited in great anticipation – the final product was printed.

Lighting a candle on the table, she placed the engraved photograph beside it, imagining every heartfelt word of this love left behind to never know what became of her one and only.

My dearest Christopher, I hope this letter eases the embers that may await you on your journey. I am sorry it is not in your English words, for I still learn to write, and I know your departure is so close. This land is so green, and the height of it above the sea is so wonderful, you could see forever the boats and anglers!

I hope you do not take too long, your family is going to grow larger soon with the child in me, and they need a father to lead them, and one to protect them. But I know you will return soon, you always have! We will spend the rest of our days in peace, as a family should, together.

I cannot wait, to meet you with our little one. If it is a son, I shall name it Hendrik after your father, and if a daughter, Leida, after my mother. Please know I shall wait forever here for you, should something happen, I will keep vigil watch over the place you led me to, Land's-End, praying for your immediate return – never to wander an eye towards another.

I will always cherish you, please hurry back my love – Aletta C.

Elizabeth dropped her head down, arms covering her head, bawling for this woman who never knew of his excruciating death, and the monster he was forced to become for god knows what purpose, except to guard some living statue. There was no more to go on, for every question led to a plot-hole, never knowing what the reason for all of this was…all the deaths going unanswered…

There was no choice left, it was time to burn down the past, and move on to elope with trauma.

Elizabeth went into the bathroom to sink as her foe did, but with head above and a half-filled lowball glass. Every sip of whiskey imbibed drove electric shocks into her head, driving her to pour the alcohol down the sink. A detoxification could only be procured via water; no more spirits, caffeine, or so much as carbonated soft drinks.

"All I want now is sleep," she said, wiping her hair out in the hallway.

The lights in her bedroom blew out from the switch causing the same quick scream she did back in the hotel, when she saw a supposed dead body of herself in the tub.

"Shit, better get a new bulb,"

She noticed every switch inoperative in the house, only natural moonlight leading the way. Seeing her computer turn off it only seemed natural, a blackout had occurred. Passing through the corridor, her peripheral vision caught an odd shape, sitting on her couch, centered in front of the large windows.

Her eyes started to adjust to the dark, thinking the winds were playing pranks on her, and the shadows of tree branches joined along.

There she saw them, two glowing meteorites of white, staring at her with full attention...

The headaches pierced her mind, the seizures took hold, and she was unable to fall – sphagnum rooted her into the hardwood. The horns appeared, its chest pushed out, proud to ensnare its prey. Images of the contorted Mountain appeared, the skull wailed, the spiked antennae attracting unknown energies, and the masses of vegetation moaning – unfortunate lives trying to break free, eyes spilling forth.

The deceitful voice rapped at the door to her mind, logic and reason vanished.

Congratulations struggler, we have known for quite some time you would survive this tribulation. Just for this moment, we speak plainly to your fallible mind. Now, we reward you with answers; answers that lead to a greater reward.

The swain had the missing additive, a vessel for transference. Longevity for a second term in the marionette, the ticking organ removed, and my gifts substituted in its place – grandiose dichotomy of what you call, the soul.

We established a melody to synchronize animal with deities, a millennium of festering organisms to breed sagacious servants, an aid to restart the building of our metropolis.

He saw it our way, until those lepers wanted to use him to quell other foreign interests – triviality. We ordered for their demise, and they fell at our gifts of phoresis, but, one took the image of the female to raze, somehow we could not predict the effects it still held over the id.

Rebellion before our fruition, we, encaged against our will, waiting for a new sacrifice to aid us – you, our struggler, have succeeded the swain. He still lives, but without at least one festered organism contained within him, he remains...immobilized, forever to float in the waters, until devoured...

Are you ready, struggler?

"What the fuck are you?!" she yelled out, more vines crawling on her.

We are nameless, the periphery of your sanity. We are the symbiosis of parasites and ancestral membranes long before yours came to being. We are of luciferin and bioluminescence – original lights inhabiting obscure pieces of art. Home, far beyond this vast; a great decision to seek another to spread our clade; perpetual war, perpetual disease, never ending, and we are deserving to feed its essence.

Gaze now struggler; inherit your place with us. Your alliances dismantled, your fears dashed into the waters, option given unto us, hear our melody, and sit in the mountain! A new transformation awaits you!

The Chimera's eyes now cracked, and for the first time, opened its mouth widely – a powerful light emitting through, revealing the colored flora produced inside it, vines shot out to entangle Elizabeth. Only the whites of her eyes were left to witness her new role.

Thorns pierced through her skin, her eyes cracking to become like the Chimera's, and the struggler evolved into a new being of flesh – the darkness hiding the full extent of her evolution.

The shrill of a newborn master echoed throughout the house, taking the Chimera to establish a new base, and with their fierce exit through the broken windows, they were lost to the forest.

None would ever find Elizabeth again…

The roaring waves crashed against the rocks, washing ashore old news. The scout was found, plucking its beak into the chest, extracting some of the self-produced flowers.

With enough at hand, it soared into the sky, marionette in its claws, and dashed it against the rocks, splitting the head. Placing the flora inside the cracks, it flew to the cliffs top.

Soon, the wails of the martyr echoed across the channel.

"I will kill it, I will find a way, and nothing will stop me. And when it is done, I will kill myself to separate my soul from this wretched puppet or my name isn't Christopher Collins!" the marionette muttered, stitching the torso.

He completed the process and awaited his body to regenerate, trying to drag it out of the strong waves before the wooden body reverted to its original state.

The waves reflected darkness cracking out of the steep cliff, the headlands hid its own monster to prey on other monsters. The vulture screeched at its image…

"A talking puppet?! You will fit perfectly in the Marchlands! The Child and that stubborn Neutral will never know how to defend themselves from you! They must learn how to die, just like your eyeless friend here! But so should you!" a distorted voice roared from the cliff.

The essence of Collins looked up to see something far more sinister surrounding the area. Tentacles of black erupted from a void of evil, his great claws ready to ensnare, the protrusion of bones waving through his body, and a smile built upon psychopathic tendencies. He went by no other name than:

The Fiend.

Soundtrack List
Nine ordeals through the peacock's eye

1. The Body – Our Souls Were Clean
2. Daughters – City Song
3. Daughters – Long Road No Turns
4. Dir En Grey – Reiketsu Nariseba
5. Opeth – Sorceress 2
6. Dir En Grey – Vinushka
7. Sleepytime Gorilla Museum – Helpless Corpses Enactment (In Glorious Times)
8. Opeth – Isolation Years
9. Torture Killer – Forever Dead

Track Placement

1. Prologue
2. Pg. 23
3. Pg. 26
4. Pg. 78
5. Pg. 81
6. Pg. 126
7. Pg. 136
8. Pg. 144
9. Pg. 150

<u>Closure</u>

I really enjoyed writing this work! Don't get me wrong it was extremely difficult for me. In the very beginning, it was just supposed to be voodoo only, but somehow archeology and evil corporations crawled in.

I didn't even have the slightest clue what my protagonist should be, and Collins was originally scripted as the only antagonist. Writing Elizabeth was so much fun, just a no-nonsense, whiskey drinking, badass with a sensitive side. Her chemistry with Hanayo grew on me, and it hurt when I had to kill off the young heir who only at the last minute realized her great fault, and their history is much like most ex-couples: filled with great joy, but something/someone new interrupted the flow.

Some people can't handle separation healthily, myself included. Just hope your ex-loves are doing OK, and wish them the best.

Also, never harm yourself or an ex if they disconnected from you…no matter how bad they did it, it'll lead to a huge regret you cannot take back!

Other than that, I'm really looking forward to October this year for my next release, the first draft is already done and most of the art is done.

Hopefully my life will get better…I miss connection.

"First, when I don't write, I'm nothing, I'm very ordinary; there's no difference between my presence and absence. I'm a restless person. Writing protects me from my nothingness and restlessness. I need to write in order to protect myself from myself." – **Ahmet Altan**; NYT 10/25/19

Disclaimer

ISBN (Paperback) 978-1-7336856-3-4

Elizabeth
Burke

Hanayo
Uesugi

Lil Puddin Taters

Original concept: Guy Maybriar
Artwork: David Hernandez
Coloring: Guy Maybriar

L-R:
Virgil - Pug
Hubert - Song Sparrow
Floyd - Tabby Cat
Caleb - Little Penguin
Gunnar - Pacific Walrus

Their "*Review*" of Miasma

Virgil: "What turd farmer would write this?! 1/5"
Hubert: "That prologue was TOO intense! 2/5"
Floyd: "Very metal, but not HEAVY METAL. 3/5"
Caleb: "Holy crap The Fiends back! 4/5"
Gunnar's Thoughts: (...Thinks stoically...5/5)

www.ingramcontent.com/pod-product-compliance
Lightning Source LLC
Chambersburg PA
CBHW022030170626
46808CB00003B/1127